Adver
Proposal

LAURA BARNARD

A CIP catalogue record for this title is available from
the British Library.

Dedication

This book is dedicated to my husband Simon who confirmed my belief that some of us do get the happy ever after. Love you!

Chapter 1

Stood up. Again. I'm getting really fucking sick of these Tinder dates. They're so bloody unreliable. I really thought this one was a nice guy, but no. It's eight forty pm, and we were supposed to meet at eight pm.

'Stood up?' A deep voice asks me.

I look up from my cocktail to see a guy at the end of the bar has spoken. Cocky bastard, assuming I've been stood up. I know his type. All light brown hair and piercing turquoise eyes. Yeah, not interested, thanks, love.

'No, actually,' I say with a smirk. 'They had a valid reason.'

'Really?' he smirks. 'What was their excuse?'

Quick, think of something.

'Mine was that she forgot she had to feed her cat.'

Oh. He's been stood up too? Who in their right mind would stand up this hunk?

I smile, lowering my walls a bit at his friendly

demeanour. 'At least she messaged you. I've got nothing.'

His eyes widen. 'You're joking? What a bastard.'

'Yep,' I nod, with a grin.

'Well...' he smiles cheekily. 'We're both here all glammed up.'

I look over his jeans and black shirt. Yes, he is. Yum.

'Why don't we get to know each other?' He gets up from his stool and moves closer, sitting on the stool next to me. Jesus, he's forward. So close that I can just about make out his refreshing citrusy scent.

I sigh, completely deflated from the evening. I could just as easily go home and crawl into my pyjamas, maybe watch a Gilmore Girls episode.

'I don't think I have the energy,' I admit with a shrug. 'I'm too old for all of this shit.'

He chuckles, his eyes lit up with humour. 'Too old? How old are you?'

'Thirty.'

He scoffs. 'That's really not old. I'm thirty-five, and I'm still young.'

I roll my eyes. 'It's different for men though, isn't it?'

He narrows his eyes in confusion. 'Why?'

'Because a man ages like a fine wine, he just gets better. A woman is like a loaf of bread—we just start going off.'

He doubles over laughing. 'No, you don't! I know plenty of fit forty-year-olds.'

I bet he does. He looks like a man whore.

'I don't mean like *that*. I mean that we're on countdown.'

'Countdown?' He frowns, his eyes burning with confusion. 'I really am clueless as to what you mean.'

'I *mean* that our time is running out. At thirty-five, our fertility basically dives off a cliff. So even if I had a baby at thirty-five, I'd still have to meet someone now.'

His eyes dart helplessly from side to side. 'Why?'

I start listing the reasons on my fingers. 'Because you have a couple of years getting to know each other, moving in with each other, then you get married and try to buy a property and then its baby time. But it could already be too late.'

He stares back at me totally bewildered. 'Jesus, woman! You make it all sound so depressing.'

I sigh heavily, feeling the weight of it all on my shoulders. 'I'm just speaking the truth. This is what most women think when they get to thirty, and they aren't in a relationship. I've lost so many friends over the years from them popping sprogs or getting married. And then there's little old me all alone. I haven't even got Sky.'

He can't suppress his laugh. 'Wow. Sounds like it's shit being a woman.'

'It is.' I grin, finding myself laughing along. 'We have it very hard.'

'Us blokes don't have it easy, you know.'

'Really?' I smirk. 'Do you know this is the third Tinder

date that's stood me up? When I tried to contact one, I found he'd blocked me!'

He narrows his eyes at me in suspicion. 'But were you stalking him?'

'No!' I shout defensively. 'I did the whole thing of trying to play it perfectly cool. I waited for him to initiate the date and pick the place and time. He took bloody ages to get round to it too.'

'Well, then he sounds like a weirdo. Jesus, did you not have a picture up?'

What has that got to do with anything?

I blink, dazed. 'Of course I did. Why?'

He gazes over my body with probing intensity. So probing, that against my better judgement I feel a shiver of excitement.

'Because surely if they saw you they'd be desperate to take you out.'

Oh my god, he's calling me hot. He's totally hitting on me.

'Unless you have a hideous personality,' he adds with a smirk. My mouth drops open at his rudeness. 'But I've been talking to you a few minutes, and I don't want to kill myself, so I'm a bit puzzled.'

I bark a reluctant laugh. 'He obviously found someone better.'

'That's the thing with Tinder.' He nods. 'Too many options. Show me your profile.'

I get my phone out of my bag and open the app, handing it over to him.

He flicks through my photos. 'Ah! Right here. Why do you have a picture of you and your cat?'

'That's freckles. He's my baby.'

He shakes his head. 'See, this just shouts crazy cat lady.'

'I'm not a crazy cat lady!' I say defensively. 'I just don't have time for a dog, and I want a companion.'

'It also probably scares guys into thinking you want to settle down.'

'Ugh! I can't win. My mates said the pics of me out partying made me look like I was up for it.'

He grimaces. 'Yeah. It is tricky. Especially when you've got less than a second to impress someone.'

'Would you have swiped right?' I can't help but ask.

He looks at me seriously for a second, as if mulling it over. Dear God, if he says no I'll die of shame.

'I haven't actually seen you on there.'

'I live just down the road in Angel.'

'Ah, I'm in West Hampstead. You're out of my three-mile radius.'

Ooh, fancy.

'Yeah, same.'

He smiles genuinely at me. 'Well if it makes you feel better, I'm fucking sick of dating.'

'Yeah, right.' I giggle. 'I bet you're the love them and leave them kind.'

'No!' He protests, but he can't help but hide the smile. 'Okay, I used to be. In my twenties, I was a bit of a nightmare, but I've grown up. These days I just feel like I don't have the time to be trying to find someone.'

'Yeah, I'm the same,' I agree. 'I just wish you could order a husband in a catalogue or something.'

'Catalogue?' he repeats, his cheeks lifting as if fighting a smile. 'Who orders anything from a catalogue anymore? It would totally be online. But...yeah, I'd probably order a wife too.'

'You know you can do that if you want a Thai bride.'

He smiles. 'Can't. Terribly racist parents,' he jokes. At least I hope he's joking. 'Have you never had a long term relationship then?'

'Yeah. I've had two long terms, but they didn't work out.'

I don't want to tell him Gary was a masturbation addict and Dave could never get it up.

'I've had one.' That shocks me. So he did once have someone he wanted to spend more than five minutes with. 'You see, I have a new theory.'

'Oh yeah.' I smile, leaning in. Being this close to him makes me feel a bit lightheaded. God, he's a gorgeous bastard. 'Go on then.'

'I think that if we'd have got married early on we'd have still been together.'

Woah. That's not the kind of thing I'm used to hearing

from a man.

'Really? Why?' I ask, bewildered.

'Because it's so much harder to leave a marriage than just a relationship. If you're married you know you're stuck with that person. It makes you try harder. You're more likely to stick out the rough patch or go to counselling. But a relationship is so easy to leave.'

I mull over his theory. I suppose he's right in a way. I'd be mortified if I had to divorce someone and would do anything in my power not to let it happen. Look at a hundred years ago—no one got divorced, they just struggled on.

'Maybe you're right,' I muse.

'I am,' he nods with a confident grin. 'And on that note, would you like a long, slow comfortable screw up against a wall?'

I spit out my cocktail. He wants to *what?* Jesus, he's forward.

'What?' I splutter, choking on the remains of my drink.

He grins widely, pointing to my cocktail. 'That's the name of your cocktail, isn't it?'

I look down at it. 'I don't know. I just told the barman to make me the most popular one on the menu.'

Humour curves his lips and then he winks. 'I bet he was looking forward to you re-ordering.'

'Cheeky bastard,' I laugh, looking back over at the balding barman. 'But yes, please, I'll have another.'

'Sorry?' he says, pretending to be puzzled. 'You're going

to have to be specific about what drink you'd like?' He smiles. I know he's enjoying this. Bastard.

I pout my lips and try to think sexy. I lower my voice, hoping it sounds husky and not like I smoke fifty a day.

'Can I please have a long, slow comfortable screw up against a wall?'

He grabs my hand and makes to leave, dragging me away with him. What?

He turns with a grin. 'Only joking. Excuse me, barman.'

~

Before we know it, everyone around us has gone home, and the barmen are washing up the glasses.

I glance at my watch. 'What time is it?'

'It's midnight,' the barman answers, clearly eager for us to leave.

'Whoops. We've chatted a bit too much.' He grins with a cheeky wink.

I don't actually know his name. I should have asked it, but the longer it went without me knowing, the weirder it felt to ask.

But my God, have we talked about everything else. About random stuff really, nothing important. Just shows we like to watch on Netflix and other such drivel like our favourite Disney films (mine is Beauty & the Beast, his is The Jungle Book), but we've just kind of gelled. There hasn't been one awkward silence, and I've felt relaxed the whole time.

Almost as if I'm chatting to a friend. A seriously hot friend that I may want to rip the clothes off.

I think he's attracted to me too. Every now and then he'll touch my thigh when he's laughing at something I said. Yeh! He thinks I'm funny, and I'm not even trying to be! I *really* hope he asks for a second date and not a one-night bunk-up. Not that I'd be strong enough to resist him.

'Shall I walk you home?' he offers with a polite smile.

Ah, bunk up it is.

'Okay,' I nod, my lady bits tingling.

He stands and takes my coat from the back of the stool, opening it up for me. It's such a cute gesture. I put my arms into it, stopping for a second to inhale his addictive scent. His hands stroke my neck from behind for a split second before he untucks my hair. It sends a shiver down my spine. Shit, I hope he didn't notice.

He puts on his coat and offers me his arm, like an old school gentleman. I laugh because I can already tell he's anything but.

We walk hurriedly down the street, the crisp December air whipping against my cheeks.

'Shit, it's freezing,' he says, pulling me closer as we walk.

'I've heard we might even get a white Christmas,' I grin. I bloody love Christmas. Even now, walking home, everything looks cheerier when in the glow of Christmas lights.

'Don't tell me, you love Christmas?'

I drop my eyes in a flush of embarrassment. 'I already have my tree up,' I admit with a smile.

He stares back at me, jaw dropped. 'What? It's the 2nd of December!'

'Exactly!' I giggle. 'I don't get the people that don't put it up until a few days before. What's the point in that?'

He shrugs. 'I don't see the point in any of it. I don't decorate at home.'

I stop walking and turn to him. 'WHAT? You don't put a tree up?'

'Nah,' he shrugs. 'Why would I? Christmas is all about parties after work and boring family gatherings at their houses.'

'I suppose,' I shrug, looking away, imagining a bare flat somewhere. 'It just seems sad.'

He snorts. 'Don't worry about me. I'm not sad. Although you probably are, getting all excited.' He digs me in the ribs to show me he's joking.

I roll my eyes. 'Whatever.'

Before I know it, we're outside my first floor flat. How's this going to go? Is he going to invite himself in? Or should I? No. No, I won't invite him in. I'm just going to go with the flow for once. Stop over analysing things.

'This is me,' I say with a shy smile.

'I can tell,' he says with a comical face, looking up at the fairy lights wrapped around the wrought iron balcony.

'It looks cute. You can't deny that.'

14

He smiles, kicking up a bit of dirt with his shoe as he faces me.

'So,' he begins, clearing his throat, 'I had a great time with you tonight. But there's something I want to ask you.'

'Yes?' I ask breathlessly.

'What's your name?'

'Oh!' I snort. God, stop snorting! 'I'm Florence, but my friends call me Flo.'

He places out his hand for me to shake. 'Nice to meet you, Florence. I'm Hugh.'

Hugh. It really suits him. I place my hand in his and shake it. It all feels so formal after the evening we've had. He surprises me by using it to pull me close to him. So, close I can feel his warm breath on my cheek.

I look up to him nervously. The friendliness in his eyes has been replaced by hunger. Oh God, I want him. Does he want me too?

As if knowing I'm uncertain, he tucks my hand into the warmth of his coat, uses his other hand to stroke my cheek and then his eyes twinkle with warmth. He lowers his lips onto mine, and quickly I feel lightheaded with lust. His lips feel soft and firm at the same time. I hang my arms around his neck. His silky soft skin is the stuff of fantasies. His tongue explores, but not in a conquering way. In more of an inquisitive, make you weak at the knees, way.

His lips finally pull away from mine, barely a breath apart. For two fierce beats of my heart, we don't move.

'Wow,' I utter out loud.

'Impressed, are you?' he asks, the edges of his mouth creeping into a smile.

'Ah, I've had better,' I joke, already aching to touch his lips again.

He reaches into his coat pocket and pulls out his phone, handing it to me. 'Here, put your number in here.'

I quickly put it in and then hand it back. I get my key out, eager to get inside. Without him wrapped round me it's bloody freezing.

His eyes fix affectionately on me. 'I'll call you.' He reluctantly lets me go.

I let myself in and give him a shy wave back. He's still there, checking I get in okay. My Mum always said that's a good sign in a man.

I run up the stairs and let myself into my flat, the twinkling fairy lights inviting me in. Who knows? By Christmas time I might just have a boyfriend.

~

'Florence!'

I wake with a start. What was that?

'Florence!'

There it is again. Where is it coming from? Am I still dreaming? I stick a toe out of my warm duvet, and the harsh reality of iciness tells me I'm awake. It's bloody freezing. I grab my phone to check the time and see three missed calls from an unknown number. What is going on? It's three am.

I begrudgingly get out of bed, quickly wrapping myself up into my big fluffy dressing gown and slippers. I follow the calling, out towards the small balcony. Who the hell is that?

I open the patio doors, the arctic air whirling into the flat. God, whoever this idiot is I'm going to kill them. I step out into the wintry night and look down. What? Hugh is looking up at me, mid calling my name.

'Hugh?' I lean over the balcony to see him clearer. 'What the hell are you doing here?'

He beams up at me. 'I'm so sorry to wake you, but I haven't been able to sleep.'

'So you thought you'd wake me?' I whisper-shout back. I don't want to wake my neighbours.

'Not just for *that* reason. I've been thinking all night and...well...I think I should just come out and say it.'

'O...kay,' I nod, bemused.

'I think we should get married.'

My eyes nearly bulge out of their sockets. He wants to *what* now?

'Are you joking?' I ask in all seriousness.

'No. I'm deadly serious.' He stares up at me expectantly. 'Look, I told you earlier how I think marriage binds you together and makes it harder to end a relationship. We like each other, we get on well, and it's clear we're sexually attracted to each other. Why not skip all of the dating crap and get to know each other as we go?'

He's serious?

'Because we could be totally wrong for each other,' I counter.

'I doubt that. And anyway, we'll always find a problem with each other eventually, but if we're married, we'll have to just learn to live with it.'

'I mean...you're really serious about this?' I check, wondering if it could be an elaborate joke.

'Yep. I think we should get married on Christmas Day. Seeing as you love Christmas so much.'

'That's only twenty-four days away! You want me to get married in twenty-four days?' I shriek in disbelief.

'Shut up!' a neighbour yells. 'Some of us are trying to sleep!'

I grimace down at Hugh. Oops.

He smiles. 'Why not? Think about it. We could be each other's happily ever after. Why wait?'

Maybe he's right. This gorgeous guy wants to be my husband. Why the hell am I even hesitating? *Because he could have severe mental health problems...*

'Wait a sec.'

I close the doors and run downstairs to meet him. As soon as I open the main door, he's there, smiling beautifully.

'So...?' he asks, a little nervously, his eyes crinkled with nerves.

Let's recap; a gorgeous man wants to marry me. Am I really going to turn him down?

I take a deep breath. 'Yes. My answer's yes.'

His smile lights up his entire face, his turquoise eyes glowing. He grabs my face and pulls me in for the most romantic, enlightening kiss I've ever experienced in my life.

Forget a boyfriend. By Christmas, it looks like I'll have a husband.

Chapter 2

Saturday 3rd December

When I wake up in the morning, I'm sure it was all a dream. That is until I open a text from an unknown number.

'Morning, wife to be ;-) Got lots to organise today. We should probably tell our parents. That's assuming you have parents alive. Lots to learn. Call me when you're awake xx

I smile to myself. He's actually crazy. I'm apparently marrying a crazy person. Which makes me a little crazy too. Maybe we *are* made for each other. But I mean, Jesus. What the hell will I tell my Mum? She's going to have me committed. And not only her but everyone. The question *how long have you been together* normally gets an answer other than 'a day'.

I push out those thoughts and call him instead.

He answers on the second ring.

'Morning, Florence,' he practically purrs down the

phone.

God, even his voice drips with sexiness.

I clear my throat. 'Morning.' I sound like a depressed frog.

'I'm guessing you're not a morning person?'

I smile to myself. 'I'm not the worst, but some prat woke me up at three am.'

'No!' he jokes. 'Don't worry. Soon you'll have a big, burly husband to tell any gentlemen callers to piss off.'

I laugh. 'Oh really. Have I agreed to marry someone else?'

'Hey!' he shouts, clearly having winded his ego. I don't know why I said it. He is big and burly. 'I might have to spank you when I see you.'

'Oh God, you're not into spanking, are you?' I ask with a cringe.

'Nah, not really. That is unless you are.'

'No thanks. My last boyfriend read Fifty Shades and thought I wanted to be beaten every time we had sex. It was beyond awkward.'

'Why didn't you just tell him you hated it?'

Because I hate confrontation.

'Because I didn't want to embarrass him.'

'Right, well that's noted. You need to be bossier in the bedroom.'

I'm glad he can't see me as I redden.

'So you wanna meet for breakfast and discuss how we're

gonna tell the parents?'

I look at the clock. It's only nine am on a Saturday.

'I'm still in bed,' I admit. 'But how do you know I'm not on my way to work?'

'You told me last night that you'd taken the month off to get ready for Christmas. Whatever that means.'

God, he has no idea about the joy of Christmas. I'm really going to have to educate him. I don't want to marry Scrooge.

'I'll need at least an hour.'

'No need.' I hear the smile in his voice. 'I'm outside.'

What? I race over to my patio doors and see him below the balcony holding up two take away cups and a bag of what I'm assuming is food.

'If this is how married life is going to be, I'm getting very excited.'

~

What a dream man. He brought us sausage and bacon rolls. Plus, he rightly guessed that I'm a coffee girl. He was shocked when I told him I take two sugars.

After a lazy breakfast on the sofa, it suddenly occurs to me that I'm wearing no makeup and must look terrifying to him.

'You must be horrified to see me without makeup,' I say, shyly.

He looked my face over. A long, lingering gaze.

'Nah. I reckon I could wake up to that every morning and not shudder in too much horror.'

I throw the napkin at him. 'Cheeky bastard.' Just how I like them.

He starts biting his lip, his eyes troubled. 'So...do you think we could get our parents together tonight to tell them?'

Oh God. This is where I have to tell him my Dad's not on the scene. 'It's only my Mum anyway.'

'Oh, your Dad not in the picture?' he asks with enquiring eyes.

'No, he left when I was four. I don't really remember him.' I shrug to let him know that it doesn't bother me.

'Crap, I'm sorry. I didn't mean to upset you.'

He's so sweet.

'No, it's fine.' I force a laugh. 'You can't miss what you can't remember.'

Now I just need to tell him that my Mum's a lesbian and will want to bring her life partner Joan.

His eyes scan over my face. 'Are you sure you're not upset?'

'No. I just...' I swallow, my throat dry. 'I need to tell you something else.'

He frowns, a comical look on his face. 'You haven't got a penis, have you?' I burst out laughing, glad for the light relief. 'Because I'm afraid that would be a deal breaker.'

I shove him on the shoulder playfully. 'No, idiot. But...' I twist my hands in my lap. 'Well...my Mum...'

He sighs heavily. 'Jesus, spit it out, Flo.'

It's the first time he's called me Flo. It feels weird.

I take a deep, steadying breath. 'My Mum's a lesbian,' I blurt out, staring down at the floor. 'Wherever we invite her, she'll want to bring her partner, Joan.'

He stares at me aghast but quickly tries to recover and act unbothered.

'No way,' he shrugs casually. 'Do you and her partner get on?'

'Sort of,' I nod. 'She's fine, and she makes my mum happy. That's the main thing.'

'That's very mature of you.' He smiles. 'Well, then we'll invite them both. How about we say eight pm at my parents' house?'

'Do you think they'd mind?' I ask with a grimace.

He snorts a laugh. 'Oh, please! They love any excuse for a party.'

'Okay,' I smile, this all still feeling unbelievably weird. 'So I guess we're meeting the parents.'

'Yep,' he smiles dreamily. 'I don't know about you, but I'm hoping they offer to help pay for the wedding. Twenty-two days doesn't give us much time to save.'

'I'd be happy with a small wedding anyway,' I insist, happy to have it just immediate family and friends.

He smiles again, but this time it doesn't meet his eyes. What is he so worried about?

Chapter 3

Hugh's invited me round his flat before we go on to his Mum's. I get the feeling he's apprehensive about me meeting her and his Dad. He avoided a lot of questions I fired at him. I get the feeling they're a bit embarrassing, like my Mum too. So, while I nervously despaired over what to wear I also baked a banana bread as a present to her. I never like to meet anyone empty handed, and everyone likes banana bread, right?

In the end, I've decided on tight black skinny jeans, Chelsea boots and a burgundy jumper top which hangs low on one side, exposing my nice shoulder. It's my favourite shoulder. I have this little freckle on it, which my Mum used to always say was adorable.

He gave me the address of his flat. It's in the posh area of West Hampstead. I wonder what he does for a living. I should *really* find that out about my future husband. I mean, hopefully, he does *have* a job. What if I've just agreed to marry some jobless slob who expects me to support him? Although I can't really imagine, morning person Hugh that lives in West Hampstead, waiting in line at the job centre.

The taxi drops me off outside an imposing, old, gated building. It looks like an old school with huge sash windows and pointed chapel-like roof. He lives here?

He buzzes me up, and I take advantage of the lift. He lives on the top floor. Of course, he does.

I knock on number 19 and wait, hopping nervously from foot to foot. God, I'm crazy going along with this. What if he's a murderer and this whole thing is a rouse so he can lure me here and chop me up into little pieces.

The door swings open, the smell of cinnamon and mandarin hitting my nostrils. Then it's his face. My god, he's beautiful. All chiselled jaw, olive skin and turquoise eyes.

The corners of his eyes crinkle. 'Hi.' He grabs me by my hand. 'Come in.'

I let myself be dragged inside. My mouth drops open when I take in the sight in front of me. Not the amazing open plan flat, with huge sash windows overlooking London, but the decorations. He's decorated it for Christmas. I thought he said he never decorates?

The whole place is dark apart from the soft glow of candles and fairy lights. In front of his fireplace is a huge pine Christmas tree with the most beautiful rose gold and cream decorations dangling from it.

'Well,' he grins, putting his arms out wide. 'What do you think?'

'You decorated?' I ask in disbelief.

He nods excitedly. 'For you.'

Am I dreaming? How is this guy actually real?

'Really?' I giggle with a snort. Sexy, *real* sexy.

'Yep. And...' He reaches into the tree and pulls out a bauble. Is he...giving me a bauble as a present?

'I got you this.'

I try to act excited and not puzzled. Then he opens up the bauble and inside is the most beautiful engagement ring I've ever seen. A huge oval soft-pink diamond is held in place by a rose gold band. There are little indentations on the band. When I look closer, I see that they're snowflakes. Oh my god. How the heck has he turned this round in a day? He must know some awesome people.

He bends down onto one knee, holding it out to me.

'Florence...' he pauses, his eyes darting from side to side. 'Is it bad I don't know the rest of your name?' he chuckles.

'It's Florence Abigail Gray,' I quickly whisper.

'Florence Abigail Gray, would you do me the honour of becoming my wife?'

I try not to smile. 'Only if you promise we can decorate like this every Christmas.'

He sighs, pretending to be exasperated at the idea. 'Go on then.'

'Then my answer is yes.'

He beams back at me, standing and removing the ring from the bauble. It's only then he seems to notice the carrier bag in my hand.

'What's this?' he asks with interest.

'Oh, I baked your Mum some banana bread.'

A smile spreads on his lips. 'Honey, you baked! Already acting like the little lady at home.'

I roll my eyes. 'I'm not going to be your *little lady*. But you're lucky that I do like to bake.'

'That's good to know.' He takes it from my hand, places it on the windowsill and slowly slides the ring onto my finger. It's a bit big, but it's so beautiful.

'Then it's official now. I put a ring on it.'

I laugh and hit him in the chest. He pulls me close to him and kisses me. God, I don't think I'll ever get bored of his kisses.

'We should probably get going now. Now...the thing with my Mother.'

I look back at him, my forehead frowning.

'What about your mother?'

'She's...she's a bit hard to take sometimes. In fact, some people would just say that she's a stuck up bitch.'

I laugh nervously. 'I'm sure she's not that bad.' I mean, I brought banana bread. I'm pretty sure she'll love me. Most parents do.

He takes my hand and squeezes it reassuringly. 'Just

remember that whatever she says, I have my own mind. And I want to marry you.'

I smile shyly. I still can't believe this stud muffin wants to marry me.

'I want to marry you too.'

~

We arrive outside the massive country house at quarter past eight. We're late. Shit, hardly a good first impression. This place is ridiculously huge.

'You didn't mention that your family are the royal family,' I joke.

He grimaces. 'I don't want this to change how you look at me. Yes, my family have money, but I'm no spoilt rich boy.'

'You do have a job then?' I joke.

'Yep. I'm a property developer. I actually developed my building and liked it so much I saved myself the best apartment.'

But he probably had a starting hand. I doubt he saved up every last penny himself.

Then it dawns on me. I'm poor compared to him. His Mum is going to hate me. And I'm wearing jeans. Fucking jeans!

'Why didn't you warn me?' I shriek, hitting him on his shoulder. 'You should have told me to dress up more. I had no idea I was meeting the Queen!'

'Don't be stupid,' he shrugs, glancing over my body. 'You look gorgeous.'

'I look fine to meet in a normal person's living room, but not a fucking palace!'

'Ooh, would you listen to that potty mouth,' he teases. 'I didn't realise I was marrying such a sailor!'

'Shut up! I'm nervous enough.' My stomach's in knots.

He takes my hand and kisses my knuckles. 'There really is no need. Remember, it doesn't matter what they think. Just me.'

'Okay...but they haven't met my lesbian mother yet.' That's when I spot her beaten up Volvo. 'Uh-oh. I spoke too soon. We need to get in there ASAP.'

He parks haphazardly, and I practically leap from the car. He grabs my hand and pulls me along after him.

'Calm down. I'm sure it's fine.'

He knocks on the door and its opened immediately by a little Filipino maid.

'Hello, Mr Humphrey.'

His name is Hugh Humphrey? My surname will be Humphrey? Florence Humphrey. I actually quite like that.

'Your mother is in the parlour.'

Parlour? Who the hell calls a sitting room a parlour? Although looking around at these huge ceilings and grandeur, I'm quickly realising this isn't your normal kind of house.

'Thank you, Sara.'

I've noticed that his whole demeanour has changed since entering the house. He's standing taller, but his shoulders are tense. Now I look at him, so is his face.

He guides me down a long hallway, his hand on the small of my back until I follow him into a magnificent room. Magnificent apart from the cold feeling which settles upon me. There's already tension in the room.

My Mum and Joan are standing together holding a glass of champagne. Across from them is a man and a woman, who I can only assume are his parents. His Mum is wearing a cream jacket with matching pencil skirt and heels. Her blonde hair is coiffed to perfection, and her perfect face is looking at me with severe distaste.

'Mother. This is Florence.'

He pulls me towards him and wraps his arm around my waist. A statement.

'Florence,' she nods politely, looking me up and down with distaste. 'How wonderful to meet you. She looks at Hugh enquiringly and I realise he hasn't explained yet.

'This is my father,' he says quickly, avoiding her question.

A tall man with a full head of grey hair smiles at me. It's a tight smile. One full of suspicion.

'I brought banana bread,' I blurt out, presenting it to his Mum. Her eyes widen in alarm as if I've just asked her did she fancy a line of cocaine. Instead, she chooses to completely ignore me and turn to Hugh.

'Hugh, we seem to have met Florence's Mother and...friend.'

'Life partner,' Joan says, pulling Mum close to her.

Oh, God. Kill me now. These are not the sort of people who seem open-minded to lesbian mothers. These look like the kind of people that hunt for sport.

'Life partner,' his Mum repeats as if she's just said pig fucking another. 'But what we're all dying to know is why we've all been summoned here.'

I gulp. She's like a scary headmistress.

Hugh takes my shaking hand in his. I look at him expectantly, waiting for him to say something.

'Err...myself and Florence...we're...' I can make out a sheen of sweat on his forehead. He coughs to clear his throat, squeezing my hand tighter. 'Getting married.'

Silence descends on the room. I stop breathing, looking around at the frozen faces. Has someone pressed pause here?

'What, darling?' his Mum repeats with a tight smile.

My Mum's features finally move, and now she looks astonished.

'Sweetheart, I didn't even know you were seeing someone. How long have you been together?'

There's the awkward question we're gonna have to get used to.

'Err...' Should I lie or tell her the truth? 'Not long.' There, that's not *actually* a lie.

'Congratulations,' his Dad says, stepping forward to shake his hand.

I'm glad *someone's* happy for us. He kisses me awkwardly on the cheek. 'Nice to meet you, Florence. My great grandmother was called Florence.'

That's a coincidence and a half. I can already tell this is his way of trying to put me at ease.   I smile gratefully.

'What, darling?' his Mum repeats, shaking her head as if just realising what's happening. 'I'm sorry, but I must have misheard you. I thought you just said you were getting married.'

His grip on my waist tightens. 'That's right, Mother. Now's the time you should be congratulating us.'

She stares back at me as if I'm the devil, her inquisitive eyes studying me suspiciously.

'Well,' Joan says with a clap, attempting to break the tension, 'we certainly wish you rainbows and moonbeams.'

I smile, despite being mortified. Why does she have to be such a hippy? Can't she just say congratulations like a normal person?

Mum smiles genuinely and gives me a quick kiss on my cheek. 'Nice to meet you,' she says to Hugh. 'Hugh, is it?'

'Yes,' he nods with a dashing smile. 'Nice to finally meet you.'

I narrow my eyes at him with a comical smile. Finally. Finally, my arse. He only knew she existed this morning.

We all look back at his Mum. The frown hasn't faded. If she carries on we're gonna have to call in her Botox guy,

33

which she no doubt has.

'I'm afraid that no, I *cannot* give you rainbows and moonbeams. I seem to be the only one here who isn't pretending that this is a joke! This is the first thing I've heard of Florence. How long have you been together? And why on earth have you kept it a secret?'

Someone was going to call us out eventually, and he did warn me about her. I look up to Hugh, biting my lip. Please be the one to answer. Don't throw me to the lions straight away.

'We met...' he swallows, but shoots me a quick reassuring smile, 'last night.'

Jaws practically hit the floor. Awkward turtle.

'Last night?' my Mum repeats. 'As in...' she tilts her head to the side, '*yesterday?*'

'Yep,' I smile, attempting to hide behind Hugh.

'Is this a joke?' His Dad asks in all seriousness.

Now that he's said it out loud it does bloody sound utterly ridiculous.

'Nope,' Hugh insists. 'Florence and I have decided that we've got the rest of our life to get to know each other.'

'This is absurd,' his Mum says in disgust. 'Why on earth would you propose to someone you just met? Have you had a breakdown, darling? Should I call Doctor Jedwards?'

They have a doctor called Jedwards? It reminds me of those nutty twins from the X Factor.

He laughs shortly, his jaw tense. 'No, mother. I'm not

having a breakdown. Just seeing things clearly for once.'

'Clearly? How on earth is marrying the first girl you set your eyes on last night thinking clearly? It's being a complete dumb arse by any standards!'

He sighs, his body deflating from effort. 'You've been banging on at me for months to settle down and get married.'

'I meant to Felicity. Not this tramp!'

Oh, my God. She actually called me a tramp?

'How dare you call my daughter a tramp?' My Mum shouts from across the room. She walks over and stands beside me. I smile at her solidarity. She might be embarrassing sometimes, but at least she trusts me to make my own decisions.

'Oh, what do you know? You big hippy lesbian!' his Mum shouts back.

'Mother!' Hugh admonishes, his eyes wide with horror.

She scoffs, hand on her hip. 'I'm sorry if I'm the only sensible one here, but I simply *cannot* accept this news. I cannot.' She throws her arms in the air. 'I refuse to give you my blessing.'

'Darling,' his Dad says, clearly trying to calm her down. 'I'm sure they're going to have a long engagement.' He looks to Hugh. 'Right?'

'Actually...' he starts, clearing his throat.

I have to help him. This is beyond awkward to watch.

'We're getting married on Christmas day.'

'Christmas day,' Joan repeats in horror. 'As in *this*

Christmas day?'

'Yes,' Hugh nods confidently. 'And we couldn't be happier.' He squeezes my waist in encouragement. I'm starting to feel like a stupid little kid for thinking we could ever get away with this, but we need to stand strong. I'm thirty-years-old for God's sakes.

His Mum's eyes nearly bulge out of their sockets. 'I refuse...'

'Luckily I'm not looking for your approval,' Hugh interrupts. 'This is my life and my decision, and I'm happy with it. You either get on board or prepare to see me far less. Now excuse me and my wife to be, we have wedding plans to get on with.'

He takes my hand and trails me behind him out of the room and down the long corridor.

'Wait, what about my Mum?' I ask, looking back into the room.

'I'm sure she can find her way home by herself,' he snaps, bad temperedly.

Wow. This is the first time I've seen him angry. It's quite intimidating. He grabs my hand again and pulls me out of the house. He opens my car door and deposits me inside before getting into his side.

I turn to face him, trying to gauge his mood. He leans his head on the steering wheel, breathing heavily.

'Are you okay?' I ask after what feels like an eternity.

He looks up, his face flushed. 'Fantastic,' he snarls

sarcastically. He quickly realises he's sounding like an arse, so smiles kindly. 'I'm sorry. I knew it would be hard, but I didn't think it was going to be that much of a disaster.'

'I suppose we did just kind of land that on them. It is kind of a weird thing to come out with.'

'Yeah, I know. I just...My Mother!' He smacks the steering wheel with both hands.

'Yeah, she's a delight,' I say sarcastically. 'Thanks for the heads up. And who's Felicity?'

He rolls his eyes. 'Just an ex-girlfriend. Don't worry, my mother didn't particularly like her anyway.'

I want to ask why they broke up but I almost don't want to know. It'll ruin the whole magic of our story.

'So anyway,' he says, taking a large deep breath. 'Do you want to look at venues tomorrow?'

I burst out laughing. Is he crazy?

'Didn't you hear them in there? They think we're insane. I can't get married if my Mum's not supporting me.'

He smiles confidently. 'Let me work on your Mum. I guarantee she'll be there at the wedding.'

I cock an eyebrow. 'You sound pretty cocksure of yourself,' I chuckle. 'What makes you so sure of yourself?'

'Come on,' he sniggers. 'You'd only met me once, and I had you agreeing to marry me.'

Dammit, he's got me there.

'Okay,' I smile, despite myself. 'But you know we have an even tougher crowd to tell, right?'

He frowns. 'Who?'

'Our friends.'

'Ah,' he nods. 'Yeah, I kind of forgot about them.'

Chapter 4

Saturday 3rd December Continued

We've each sent group texts round to our mates asking them to meet us at a bar in London. They were all suspicious, so we had to tell them that we had news. They've been speculating ever since. Job promotion, pregnant, new boyfriend—they've gone through them all. Funnily enough, none of them guessed I'd be married by Christmas.

'Ready?' Hugh asks, grasping my hand.

I look down at it. Is it weird that holding his hand already feels like the most natural thing in the world? I take a deep inhale. 'As I'll ever be.'

'Hey.' He stops walking and lifts my chin with his finger. 'I know you're nervous, but they'll be fine.'

'Really?' I smile with raised eyebrows. 'You must have seriously chilled friends.'

'Nah, they're gonna try and have me committed. Make sure to stop them, or we'll never get down the aisle.' He plants a quick kiss on my lips.

God, he's dreamy.

'Okay,' I smile.

We walk into the bar, the electric jazz buzzing in the background. I spot my friends on a chesterfield sofa in the corner—their faces lit up by tea light candles.

'Meet you over there?' I ask with a shy smile.

'Course,' he smiles, squeezing my hand. 'Prosecco?'

'Keep em coming.'

I rush over to the girls. I have three close-knit friends: Nadine, Kelly, and Mia. Nadine was my next door neighbour growing up, Kelly I met at my first job, and Mia is an old roommate.

'Hey, bitches,' I greet them fondly with a smile.

'Here she is,' Nadine smiles. 'Took your time, love.' She hates me even being a couple of minutes late. Typical schoolteacher.

Kelly and Mia jump up to give air kisses.

'So,' Mia says with a wicked glint in your eye, 'what the hell is this news?'

'Yeah, talk about keep us in suspense,' Kelly chuckles, draining her glass of rose.

'It's...kind of a long story,' I say with a grin, looking down at the floor.

I really want Hugh with me when I tell them. You know, so they don't just book me straight into an asylum.

'But, seriously,' Nadine says, her hand on my arm. 'Are you pregnant? Because I didn't even think you were seeing

40

anyone?'

'Um...'

'Ladies!' a voice booms over us.

I turn round to see Hugh with a tray of drinks. Thank God, he's finally here. I smile, feeling a sense of calm waft over me. How is it I've only known him a few days and already he makes me feel better about everything? He must be an expert handler.

'I took the liberty of ordering you another round.'

Ah, he got the girls drinks? Clever guy.

'Thanks, but we're not interested,' Mia says rudely. 'We're just having a girlie night.'

I raise my eyebrows at Hugh, unable to hide my smile.

'No, girls, this is the news I was talking about. This is Hugh.'

He places down the tray of drinks and then gives me a quick peck on the lips.

Kelly's eyes nearly pop out of their sockets.

'And these are my friends,' he says gesturing to two guys behind him. 'Jace,' he explains nodding to a tall, good looking blonde, 'and Troy.' A black guy with a huge afro and hipster glasses smiles back.

His name can't seriously be Troy, can it? Do people call their children that?

'Hi,' Mia says, smiling apologetically.

The guys sit down between them.

'So,' Troy says, clapping his hands, leaning forward on

41

his knees. 'What's this big news? That you guys are together now?'

'Yeah, I thought you only had a date Friday night,' Nadine says suspiciously. 'A bit early to be announcing yourselves as a couple, isn't it?'

Uh-oh. I look at Hugh, my eyebrows raised so high they're basically touching my hairline. She thinks it's too soon for a relationship? Wait until she hears about the engagement.

'What can I say,' he smiles, taking my hand in his. 'When you know, you know.'

I take a large gulp of Prosecco.

'Well, I'm happy for you,' Kelly says, raising her new glass of Rose at me. 'Great news.'

I clear my throat. I have to get this over and done with as quickly as possible.

'That's not all of the news,' I admit.

Mia gasps. 'I knew it! You *are* pregnant!'

'They only met the other night, dickhead,' Nadine snaps. 'That'd be the fastest conception in history.'

'Oh yeah,' she frowns, slumping back down on the sofa.

I look to Hugh for help. He smiles reassuringly before turning back to address them.

'We're also...getting married.'

Blank faces greet us. I look from face to face expecting a reaction. Any minute now.

Jace starts laughing. 'You're joking, right?'

We both shake our heads.

'Look,' Hugh starts, 'we know it's sudden, but we're hoping you can get behind us, as our friends, and be excited for us.'

'Excited for you?' Nadine shrieks. 'Are you fucking nuts?'

'I mean...' I fidget with my hands, 'maybe a little, yeah. But...I'm still doing it.'

'Are you a foreigner?' she barks at Hugh.

'What?'

'Is that what it is? You need a green card or something? Because I'm sure there are other far dumber girls out there willing to help you. Don't fuck around with our girl, Florence.'

'Woah,' he says with a large puff of air. 'I don't need any card. I'm completely self-sufficient. I just want someone to spend my life with.'

'And you thought that was her?' Troy asks in disbelief.

Wow, that hurt.

'Hey!' Mia says in outrage. 'Don't you dare be rude to my friend.'

'Sorry, it's just, Hugh, I've seen you with lots of women and—' he points to me.

'Don't fucking dare finish that sentence,' Hugh warns him. 'You haven't even spoken to Florence.'

'Have you?' Jace asks with a bemused grin. 'Because I've spoken to my dentist more than I reckon you've had time

43

to chat to her since Friday.'

'I agree,' Kelly says. 'I'm all for a big romantic gesture, but getting married?'

'Yeah, but I assume it's going to be a long engagement?' Mia asks with enquiring eyes.

'Not...exactly,' I admit. 'We're getting married on Christmas day.'

'Christmas fucking day?!' Nadine and Troy seem to shout at the same time.

'Yep,' I nod.

Nadine stands up and takes me by the arm. 'Excuse us everyone while I talk to my girl in private.' She drags me up to standing.

I allow her to lead me into the corner. 'Ok, Florence. What the fuck is up? Have you had a breakdown or something? I mean, I know he's hot—but married? What if he's a fucking psycho?'

I smile. 'But what if he's not? What if he's a beautiful man with a great personality that for whatever reason wants to marry me?'

She stares back at me. That's stumped her.

'I just...are you serious? By Christmas day?'

'Yes, and I was going to ask you to be my maid of honour. But if you don't approve...'

'I'll do it,' she interrupts, sighing as if it's a massive inconvenience. When I know deep down she's peeing her pants in excitement of being asked. 'Of course I'll do it, but promise me something.'

'Yep,' I nod with a comical grin. 'First born will be called Nadine.'

'Shut up,' she laughs, shoving me on the shoulder. 'No, promise me that from now until Christmas day you'll truly consider if this is a good idea. If you have any doubts, *any* doubts whatsoever, you won't marry him.'

'That's fine,' I nod. 'Believe it or not, I get how crazy this is, but I mean, look at him.'

We look back at Hugh who's already got the others laughing along to some story he's telling. I knew he'd win them over.

'Okay, he is kind of dreamy,' she admits, a smile escaping.

I sigh, almost swooning as I look at him. 'And he's going to be my husband.'

Chapter 5

Sunday 4th December

The night actually ended up going fabulously after the initial shock. We drank a fuck load of alcohol and ended up in a club. The last time I glanced at my watch it was just after two am and then it gets a bit fuzzy.

I was glad when I woke up this morning and found that Hugh hadn't slept over. I don't want the first time we have sex to be something I don't remember.

He's there, on my doorstep at seven am with a coffee for me.

'God, you're such a morning person,' I grumble, letting him follow me up the stairs.

'I thought we could start with the wedding planning,' he grins, cheerfully. 'No time like the present.'

'Let me wake up at least,' I grunt.

'Aren't you girls supposed to lap this stuff up? Don't you have a Pinterest board with our entire wedding already planned?'

I look back at him to check if he's being serious. He seems like he's genuinely expecting an answer.

'Er...no.'

He gives a lopsided smile. 'I knew there was a reason I chose you.'

I scoff. Chose me? I'm not some bloody prize to be selected.

'We *chose* each other. Don't make out I'm the lucky girl you selected, and you're God's gift to women.'

'Oooh!' he jokes with a wicked grin. 'Someone's *really* not a morning person.'

I take a deep breath and try to collect myself. Mustn't be a bitch. He might not marry you.

'I'm fine. I'll get a notepad.'

I quickly splash my face with water, apply some deodorant and pinch my cheeks. That'll have to do. I'm far too hungover to bother with makeup.

'Sorry about the no makeup,' I apologise as I walk back out with a notepad. 'But I suppose you'll have to get used to it.'

He snorts a laugh. 'Luckily for me you're not a monster.'

I roll my eyes with a smile. 'You say the sweetest things.'

Then I realise. I'm assuming we're going to live with each other as man and wife. Has he thought about that?

'Um...we haven't even talked about where we're going to live.'

47

'Yeah,' he nods. 'I suppose we should talk about that.' He raises his eyebrows comically. 'Your place or mine?'

I look around my beloved flat. It's taken me years to get it looking just how I like it.

'Well...I do love my place...'

He scrunches up his face in distaste. 'Bit girlie though, isn't it?'

I suppose my taste *is* a bit girlie, but I haven't had to please anyone but me.

'With your stuff in it, it'd look more masculine.'

'Don't you like my place?' he asks, putting on puppy dog eyes. 'I mean it's brand new, top of the range. The places are going for half a million.'

Ugh, god. He's all about the money.

'Yeah, but...it's not got much character, has it?'

'What do you mean?'

How do I put it politely?

'I mean every flat is exactly the same. I prefer to make it personalised. You should have seen this place when I first bought it.'

He chews on his lip, looking around. 'It's not big enough though, is it?'

'Big enough for what? There's only two of us. Anyway, it's cosy.'

'Cosy's the word,' he smirks. 'And that's two adults before we start thinking about a family.'

48

'Woah, woah, woah! Who said we're having a family straight away?'

Has he been planning our future without consulting me?

'Well, not *straight* away, but you said yourself you need to get a move on.'

I splutter out a laugh. The cheeky fucker!

'Yeah, but I want to get to know you a bit better first! Jesus, is it not enough I'm marrying you, now you want me popping sprogs out the minute we're across the threshold?'

He stifles a laugh. 'No, of course not. I'm just saying would it not make sense for us to both sell up and buy a house together that will do us for the next couple of years?'

I suppose when he puts it rationally like that it does sound like a good idea.

'Yeah, you're right.' I look around at my beautiful flat. 'I'm just gonna miss this place.'

'I'll miss mine, too,' he reminds me softly, 'but we'll get something we both love.'

I think of his ultra-modern flat and my chintzy shabby chic style. Hmm, I can already see a big compromise to be made there.

'Anyway, back to the wedding,' he says, pointing at the notepad.

'Right.'

'First thing we should do is write a guest list.'

49

'Okay,' I nod. 'Let's do this.'

~

Three hours later and our list is complete. We've got eighty-two people, which we're both happy with. Any more than that and it'll be too big. We've both agreed we want to keep it as intimate as possible. Apart from that, we're pretty clueless. We're not sure what kind of venue we want, what kind of colours or even what kind of cake.

In the end, we agreed to do a Christmas theme. It should be easy, as most places will be decorated up for it anyway. It helps that I love this time of year. God, whenever I think that I'm getting married I lose my breath. This is really happening. My friends are right. This is insane.

'I think we should call in re-enforcements,' I announce, my head whirling with everything we have to do.

'Do you mean our...mothers?' he gulps comically.

I grimace. 'I think it's a bit too soon for them. They're probably still a bit angry. I was thinking more Nadine. Now *that's* a girl that's got her entire future wedding on Pinterest.'

He smiles fleetingly. 'Okay, sounds great. But one thing we haven't talked about is budget.'

'Ah.'

'Yep. Most of my money is tied up in property, and if I'm honest I don't want to ask my Mother.'

God, I'd rather die than ask her.

'Yeah, I know the father of the bride traditionally pays,

but we'd have to find him first.' I have a little chuckle to myself at my hilarious joke.

He frowns, his eyes darting helplessly from side to side. 'Your Mum doesn't know who he is?'

God, he thinks my Mum was a whore.

'Yes!' I shriek. 'Of course she knows who he is. But he got up and left when I was four years old.'

'Why did he leave?'

'Beats me,' I shrug. 'Said he was going out for a pint of milk apparently and just never came back.'

His face contorts. 'Shit. Did you check he wasn't hit by a car or something?'

I nod, sick of hearing the same questions I've heard all my life. 'She called all the hospitals. Apparently, he just went. It's no big deal. I don't remember him.'

'I'm sorry anyway.' He smiles sincerely.

'Either way, my Mum doesn't have a pot to piss in. She's not got any money to offer, and I'd hate to have to ask her. But I have about four grand in savings.'

'Cool. I have three, so together that's seven. That can do a wedding, right?'

'I bloody hope so.'

~

'Seven grand?' Nadine repeats, her face twisted in horror. 'You want me to plan an *entire* wedding for seven measly grand? And we have less than a month to plan it. It's official. You've lost your minds.'

'Come on,' Hugh pleads, taking a sip of his coffee. 'Seven grand must get us *something*.'

'It's going to be very hard,' she argues sternly. 'Let's see.' She gets some papers out of her large handbag. 'When you called and said you have eighty-two guests I shortlisted venues that are still available and can cater to that number. Hmm.' She turns the piece of paper over and starts scrawling.

'Okay, so let's say a grand for the dress,' she writes down.

'Woah,' Hugh and I both say at the same time.

'A grand for a dress?' he repeats in shock. 'That's fucking ridiculous.'

She glares at him before turning to me. 'Florence, this is going to be the most important day of your life. Don't you want to look amazing?'

I shrug. 'Yeah, but surely I can look amazing in a dress for a couple of hundred.'

She raises her eyes but begrudgingly writes down £500 for the dress. 'I think you'll change your mind, but okay, whatever. Let's put down £250 for the men's suits.'

'Woah!' Hugh jumps in. 'My suit alone will be that much.'

'Why don't you ask the men to get their own suits?' I ask. 'I was thinking of asking the bridesmaids to do it as a wedding present to cut costs.'

Nadine nods. 'That won't be a problem with us.'

'But...men are different,' he moans, shifting uncomfortably. 'I don't want to look like a poor bastard.'

'Right,' Nadine continues, ignoring him. 'Officiants are normally around £500 and photography you can get for around a grand. Do you guys want a DJ or a band?'

'Ooh, I'd love a band,' Hugh says eagerly, his face lit up like a kid at Christmas. 'Something really cool.' He turns to me. 'That okay with you?'

'Yep,' I nod. So far so easy.

'Okay,' Nadine scribbles, '£1,500 for a band. Let's see—rings will be £500 minimum and even if you have the bare minimum flowers you're talking £500.'

'£500 for flowers?' I shriek. 'I don't even particularly like flowers!'

'Babe, it's a wedding,' she tries to reason as if I'm a child in her class. 'You need flowers.' She looks back down at her list. 'Invitations you're looking at about £250.'

'Fuck off!' I shout, several people in the coffee shop turning around to stare at me.

'Darling,' Hugh grins, 'I didn't realise you were such a potty mouth.' He chuckles uncontrollably, clutching his sides in agony.

'Sorry, but £250 for a bit of paper. That's ridiculous!' I whisper.

'I have to agree,' he nods, now serious again. 'Can't we just send out an email or something?'

Seems a good idea to me.

'An email?' Nadine repeats, her brows snapped together. 'Are you serious? You're going to send out an e-invite for your bloody wedding?'

'Why not,' I shrug. 'If it saves us wasting that money.'

She sighs as if we're a massive inconvenience. Err, it is *our* wedding.

'Okay. But we still have transport, cake, hair, and makeup to sort out.'

'My buddies have some nice cars. I'm sure they can sort us out,' Hugh replies, already getting his phone out to text someone.

'And my Mum can make the cake. She's actually good at it. And obviously, I'll just do my own hair and makeup.'

She stares at me for a long time. So long in fact, that I wonder if I should say something.

'Riiiiiiight. So, you're sending e-invites, and you're doing your own hair and makeup.' She scribbles on her sheet. 'So that leaves…£2,250 for the wedding reception.'

Shit. Hugh looks at me with raised eyebrows. That doesn't sound like enough.

She goes through her papers, throwing sheet after sheet down on the table until she stares at one for a long time, a permanent line appearing between her eyebrows. She hands it over.

'I actually put this one in for a joke. But it seems it's the only one you can afford.'

I look down at the pub on the sheet. It looks old and

grotty.

She grimaces, but attempts to force a smile. 'Okay, so....good luck.'

Chapter 6

Hugh pulls into the car park—the parking lines so faded you can't make them out. I look up at the grotty pub. I can't believe I'm going to have to get married in this shit hole. I suppose there's nothing actually wrong with it, apart from the dirty windows and peeling paint. I just never imagined having my wedding reception in a pub. Especially one called The Duck and Goose. But I suppose I never imagined getting married to a near stranger either.

'So…I'm guessing when you dreamt of your wedding you didn't imagine a pub?' he asks good-humouredly.

How is he able to read my mind? I've dated people for months, and they've never been this in tune with me.

'Not exactly,' I admit, forcing a smile. 'But if this is all we can afford then we need to make the best of it.'

'That's my girl,' he grins, opening his door.

I don't know why, but it feels weird him saying that. Am I even his girl yet? If this were a normal date, I wouldn't dare call him my boyfriend, let alone fiancée. The thing that's niggling at me more than anything is that we haven't had sex yet. Haven't done anything like that in fact.

We haven't actually kissed passionately since the first night we met. I know they say marriage is about a lot more than sex, but what if we're not sexually compatible? What if he has a weird shaped dick? Or a tiny dick. God, I really need to investigate before I say I do.

My door opens, breaking me from my worries. I absolutely love how he always opens the door for me. His mother might be a monster, but at least she raised him right.

'M'lady,' he jokes, holding out his hand.

I take it. 'Why, thank you, good sir.'

We walk towards the front door. It really hasn't got kerb appeal. The flowerpots have half-dead flowers in there, and the brickwork has been patched up poorly in areas.

A big burly man covered in tattoos opens the door before we have a chance to knock.

'Hi there!' he booms in a loud, confident voice. 'I assume you're the love birds looking to get married here?'

'Possibly,' I say quickly, eager not to confirm anything.

'Well, quick, come in from the cold.'

At least he's friendly. We hurry into the dark, dim pub. I shiver; if it's possible, it's actually colder in here. I look around as the mildew smell creeps up my nostrils. There's nothing particularly wrong with it. There's a long bar in the middle with tables darted around and a small extension out the back. It's just that it's a pub. No sweeping staircase or grand marble. Okay, maybe I have dreamt of my wedding before. I guess I always imagined pure luxury, not a place that does two-for-one shots.

A woman with her blonde hair in curlers comes in. 'Hi, loves! Would you like a cuppa?'

'I'm fine, thanks,' Hugh and I both say at the same time.

Okay, focus on the positives. They're lovely people.

We sit down, and Hugh starts discussing all the finer details. I can't help but retreat into my own head. I'm starting to think we should wait longer and do this properly. I don't want to look back at my wedding album and regret not having done it right.

On the way out Hugh takes my hand. 'I know you hate it.'

'I don't hate it,' I say quickly. I don't want him to think I'm a spoilt brat. 'I just don't love it.'

He smiles sadly. 'I know. We do have other options, you know?'

'Really?' I can't help but ask hopefully. Has he been holding out on me?

He grimaces. 'My mother.'

~

Tuesday 6th December

So, that's how I find myself sat across from her in the posh manor house she arranged to meet us at the next day.

'Can I take your order?' a waiter asks, saving me from the awkward silence.

'Yes,' she says without a smile. 'We'll have a bottle of prosecco.'

A woman after my own heart. Maybe we *can* be friends.

'And...' she scans down the menu. 'Three La Truite's.'

Hugh rolls his eyes. This must be a regular occurrence.

I quickly scan down the menu to see that it's a trout fillet.

'Um...I don't actually like fish,' I say apologetically.

She stares at me like I just spoke in tongues. 'Don't tell me you're one of those vegans?' she asks, clear disgust in my voice.

I shake my head, trying to contain a giggle. 'No. I just don't like fish.'

'I didn't know that about you,' Hugh muses, taking my hand under the table. 'Still so much to learn.'

His mum snorts. 'Well, that's what happens darling when you decide to marry someone after five minutes.'

'Mother,' he warns, glaring at her. 'You promised you'd play nice.'

'And I am, darling!' she says, playing innocent. 'In fact, I want to know more about you, Florence. So, let's see, we already know that your mother's a lesbian and that you're marrying my son, but apart from that I have nothing.'

I chance a look at Hugh. He smiles back apologetically, but I see him lean in, eager to see what I'm going to say.

'Um...I'm a freelance makeup artist.'

'Ah, so you're used to weddings, then, I take it,' she says with a smug smile.

'Actually, I don't do weddings. I work more on movies sets and with celebrities. In fact, I've just finished working with Estee Lauder for their latest campaign.'

Her mouth pops open ever so slightly. That shut her up.

'That's why I've given myself the month of December off. So I can relax and get ready for Christmas.'

'Oh, I see. You've done well for yourself.'

I can't believe she's giving me a compliment.

'Considering you were raised by a single mother.'

There we go. That's more like it. I look to Hugh. Has he told her my Dad left or is she just assuming? Why does she make that sound like a bad thing anyway? It's not her fault my Dad left.

'You can't have had much money growing up.' She re-arranges her features, attempting to look concerned, but I can still see she has a separate agenda.

I think back to my Mum working two jobs, spending her spare time cutting coupons out of our neighbour's magazines.

'Things were tight, but my Mum worked hard. Made sure I never went without.'

That's a total lie. I went without a lot. So did she. I can remember her having cereal for dinner because she could

60

only afford to feed me properly, but I don't want her knowing that. It would sound like I'm slagging her off when she's the best mum in the world.

'She must be very proud of you.'

Wow, a compliment. It sounds genuine. I don't quite know how to take that. Maybe she *is* trying to be nice. Maybe this is her...trying.

'And on the subject of money...' she shuffles around in her bag and removes some papers, 'I spoke to the family solicitor and got this written up.'

She goes to hand it to me, but Hugh snatches it off her. 'What the hell is this?' he snaps, his ears growing red with fury.

'What is it?' I whisper, attempting to look at it.

'Don't overreact, darling,' she says to Hugh. She turns to me. 'It's just a little chat about protecting my son.'

'Mum,' he growls, dropping the paper to the table. 'This is out of order.'

I crane my neck to see the title. 'Prenuptial Agreement.'

Shit. She thinks I'm running off with his money? I can't help but stare back at Hugh, eyes wide, no doubt looking like a deer in the headlights.

'Florence had no idea I had any money whatsoever when we met, unlike most women I go out with.' He smiles warmly at me. 'I'm not making you sign it.'

Thank God for that.

'Just take a moment to think, darling,' she warns,

61

casting her accusing gaze at me. 'You're rushing ahead with this *'wedding'*. Let me at least protect your assets. And not just yours, but ours.'

I feel like I should speak. Stand up for myself.

'Just for the record, I'm not after any money.' She looks back at me suspiciously, eyebrows raised. 'I plan on making this marriage work, so by all means, I'll sign it.'

Hugh's mouth drops open. 'Are you sure, Flo?'

He actually looks a little relieved, which hurts my feelings. I know it shouldn't, but it does. I want him to fight for me and by me signing this it's almost as if we're giving up before we've even started.

I shrug as if it doesn't bother me. 'No big deal.'

If I have to get divorced because this was all a rushed mistake, that will be the devastating factor, not that I can take all of his money.

'Marvellous.' His Mum claps.

'Although...I should take this home for my Mum's partner Joan to look over.'

She rolls her eyes. 'Why? Do lesbians also specialise in contracts?'

'Mother!' Hugh shouts, his turquoise eyes flashing with disgust.

'I'm not sure,' I snarl back sarcastically. 'But she used to be a solicitor so I should take her advice. Lesbians can also hold down jobs, you know,' I add sarcastically.

She rolls her eyes. 'When they're not licking vagina's,'

she whispers bitchily under her breath.

Is this woman for real? She's beyond vulgar.

'Come on,' Hugh insists, taking my hand. Anger radiates off him. 'Let's go. We don't have to listen to this.'

'Really?' his mother snarls. 'So you didn't both ask me here today for money?'

Dammit, she's got us there. I look to Hugh, discreetly raising my eyebrows.

'We were going to ask for help with the wedding,' Hugh admits quietly, so as not to draw attention to us. 'But we don't need it. We'd rather get married in a shitty pub than have you hanging over us the entire time.'

He takes my elbow and guides me out of the restaurant. A guy that's not a mummy's boy? He's a keeper.

Chapter 7

Wednesday 7th December

I wake up the next morning to someone banging on my door. Ugh. I cover my head in the duvet and pray they'll go away. I'm not waiting for a delivery. I'm supposed to be using this time off work to relax, but instead, I'm planning a wedding. I at least deserve to lie in, don't I?

But the persistent fucker keeps banging. Ugh. If it's a Jehovah's Witness, I will smack them in the face. I drag myself out of bed and stomp angrily down the stairs. I swing the door open.

'What do you want?' I snarl.

Looking back at me is the devastatingly handsome Hugh. He's leaning against my doorframe in a navy suit and white shirt unbuttoned at the neck, showing just a glimpse of his tanned skin. When my eyes eventually travel back up to his face, I see that his lip is quirked in amusement.

'Morning, sunshine. Like something you see?'

I quickly try to take the sleep out of my eyes. I must look

like a bloody monster.

'Err...no,' I mumble quickly, tucking a bit of hair behind my ear while blushes spread on my cheeks.

'Really?' he smiles, amused.

'What's so bloody urgent anyway? You *really* need to stop waking me up so early, or I'm gonna end up dumping your arse.'

He walks past me up the stairs. Oh, do come in. God, he's annoying.

I begrudgingly follow him, stomping my feet noisily. When I find him, he's in the kitchen boiling the kettle and spooning coffee into my mugs. Okay, so I'm slowly forgiving him.

I cross my arms and lean against the counter. 'So...are you going to tell me why you woke me up so early?'

'Ah, yes.' He reaches into his pocket and produces an envelope, handing it over to me. 'Take a read.'

I look down the posh looking thick card.

> *Mr and Mrs Humphrey*
>
> *Request the pleasure of your company*
>
> *At Florence Gray and Hugh Humphrey's*
>
> *Engagement Party*

'What? Did...did we just get invited to our own engagement party?'

He nods, handing over my coffee. 'Yep.'

'But we don't even know about this. We told your Mum we don't want her money.'

He chews on his bottom lip. 'I know. It's probably some kind of trick. Like, show us what we could have.'

I place it on the counter and sigh. 'I'm only used to men playing games. I'm not used to their mothers getting involved too.'

He snorts a laugh. 'You've clearly never met mine.'

I attempt to rub the rest of the sleep out of my eyes. 'So why don't we just tell her we don't want it?'

He grimaces. 'I've already had twenty people contact me congratulating me and confirming they'll attend.'

I catch on quickly. This could be embarrassing for him to cancel.

'And it will be really awkward if we then have to tell them the party isn't happening,' I finish for him.

He nods with a shy shrug. 'I know it's out of order, but maybe we should just go along with it for now?'

Ugh. I can already see this is how it's going to be. His mother controlling every situation. I feel exhausted at the thought of it.

I sigh, desperate to be back in my bed. 'Look, I don't mind. When is it?'

'Tomorrow.'

'Tomorrow,' I repeat. Hang on. 'TOMORROW? Are you insane? How the hell am I going to get ready in that time?'

He looks at my hair. 'Yeah, maybe get started on your hair right away,' he chuckles.

'Ha ha,' I snap, sticking out my tongue.

'But seriously, you don't take twenty-four hours to get ready for a party, do you? Because I need to know if most of my married life is going to be spent waiting.'

'No, of course not. I just...' I swallow, attempting to shove down the panic. Should I be honest and tell him I'm scared? 'I'll need to buy a new dress.' Chicken shit.

'Then we'll go shopping.'

I look back at him with raised eyebrows. 'Really? *You* do shopping?'

'Not exactly,' he admits, 'but I can come with you and introduce you to a personal shopper I know well.'

I think about my current wardrobe of jeans and wrap dresses. They're definitely not going to cut it.

'Okay. But, can I have another hour in bed first?'

He raises his eyebrows. 'Only if I can come in with you?'

I nearly pass out from shock. Shit, is he serious? He wants to have sex...now? The first time when I look this rough and I'm this tired?

'We can just spoon,' he adds with a smile. 'No need to look so terrified.'

'No, sorry. It's just...I'm nervous about...you know, that.'

'What?' he questions, eyebrows knitted together.

'Us having...you know...sex.'

He laughs heartily. 'Then maybe we should get it out of the way.'

He strides over to me and takes my face in his hands. He pauses for a beat before pulling my lips up to meet his. It shocks me so much my breath is stolen, and I almost stumble.

My shaking hands find their way into his hair and before I can reason with myself I'm gripping his hair roughly, so rough he bites my lip.

'Ow!' I yelp.

He grins back at me. 'I take it you're not into any kinky shit then?' he chuckles.

Dammit, I don't want him to think I'm boring.

'Err, yeah...but you just...caught me off guard.'

He pulls me back in for a quick peck on the lips. 'You're so adorable.'

I roll my eyes. 'That's what every girl wants to hear,' I drawl sarcastically.

Dammit. Why did I have to ruin the mood?

I take a deep breath and kiss him again. He strokes the side of my face tenderly.

'We don't have to do this now,' he reasons, pulling back and gazing down at me.

'No, I want to,' I press. 'It's better if we just get it over and done with.'

His eyes nearly pop out of their sockets. Oops, wrong thing to say.

'That's not what I meant. I'm just nervous,' I admit reluctantly.

He takes my shoulders in his hands. 'Florence, we shouldn't want to get this over and done with. I get that you're nervous. We're still getting to know each other.'

'But we're getting married in less than 18 days!'

He smiles reassuringly, stroking my cheeks with his thumbs. 'Why don't we leave it until our wedding night?'

'Huh?' Is he bloody serious? I'm no virgin.

'Leave our first time until our wedding night,' he explains calmly.

'You're crazy!' I laugh. 'What if we're sexually incompatible?'

'Then we'll just work on it,' he counters like it's no big deal. Like it's not the rest of our lives.

'What if I'm shit in bed?'

He eyes light up with amusement. 'Are you?'

Shit, am I?

'I don't bloody know! I don't have sex with me, but I'm single. That could be telling me something!' I realise I must sound hysterical, but I'm clearly more freaked out about this than I thought.

He shakes my shoulders slightly. 'Flo, calm down. You're just freaking out. It's normal. I seriously doubt you'll be shit in bed, especially when you kiss like that.'

I look down, in a flush of embarrassment.

'I...' It's pretty rare that I'm speechless.

'Let's just go shopping and get you a pretty dress, okay?'

I nod. Yeah, let's go shopping. That will get rid of my

problems.

~

He drives past the turning for the local shopping centre. 'Where are we going?' I ask, studying his face, trying to read him.

He gives me a fleeting broad grin before turning back to the road.

'I know this little boutique.'

Oh God. Great. More stuff out of my comfort zone.

About five minutes later he pulls up outside a small green-fronted shop in an area I've never been to before.

'This is it. Supposed to be the best place in town.'

I look up at it. It hardly looks amazing. Faded gold writing tells me it's called The Closet. Where the hell did he hear about this place? I'm sure it's not as posh as it looks.

He opens my door for me and takes my hand. Every time he touches me it's as if an electric current goes up my arm.

I take a discreet deep breath as he opens the huge green door.

Wow. I was wrong. Everything in here is so grand. Rows and rows of gold rails hold the most spectacular dresses. I step onto the plush cream carpet suddenly worried my heels are dirty. It smells so clean and fresh in here. I hope I don't suddenly have the urge to fart.

A quick look around tells me this is exclusively a

woman's shop. How the hell does he know about this place?

'So, how come you know about a woman's boutique?' I ask with a badly hidden scrunched up face.

'Do you really want to know?' he asks with a quirked up eyebrow.

I frown. Does that mean he's had loads of women? Shit, maybe I'm just one of many girlfriends he's promised the world to only to—then get bored of and dump.

'Hugh!' an elderly woman dressed impeccably in a cream suit shrieks, rushing out from the back room. 'How are you?' She air kisses him and then takes his hands, holding him at arm's length to appraise him. 'I hear you're engaged!'

He smiles fondly at her. He must like this woman. I straighten my shoulders and smile.

She turns to me. 'I take it you're the lucky girl,' she gushes, pulling me in for a hug.

Wow. She's bloody friendly. If only his Mother could be half as affectionate.

'Martha,' he says, fondly, 'this is the lovely Florence.'

'And lovely she is,' she smiles so wide I'm worried her face is going to break apart. 'I didn't even know you were seeing someone.'

'It's...fairly new,' he admits, winking at me.

I blush like a schoolgirl.

'A whirlwind romance?' she fawns, practically jumping up and down on the spot. 'How romantic!' She turns her attention to me. 'Now! It's time to find something fabulous for your engagement party.'

Ah. She must be invited too.

She scans over my body with critical eyes. I cross my hands over my chest, feeling exposed.

'Okay, so you're a twelve. Come, come. We'll get you started.' She takes my hand and starts pulling me towards the back changing rooms.

Hugh follows, already tapping away on his phone. I've obviously lost him to his emails.

'Do you need to be somewhere?' I ask sarcastically. I pout to let him know I'm only half joking.

'Doesn't matter,' he shrugs. 'I'm not leaving you.'

'Isn't he just wonderful,' Martha says on a swoon. 'I'll get my assistant to fetch you some drinks while I get some dress choices. If you could just strip down to your underwear and I'll be back in a tick.'

What now? Strip down to my underwear?

I stare back at Hugh. 'Is she serious?'

'You heard her,' he grins, opening the curtain to a small changing room. 'Strip.'

I stare at him, trying to work out if he's serious. His smirk tells me he's expecting me to decline, but that just makes me want to shock him. I need to show him I'm not some cowering little flower. It's weird, but just knowing we're not having sex until the wedding night now gives me the confidence to sex it up a bit.

I walk past him but pause before he has a chance to draw

72

the curtain.

'Can you help me?' I ask seductively over my shoulder.

I tilt my head forward, looking down so I can't gauge any kind of reaction from him. The pause makes all previous bravado dissolve. I can't bear the possibility of rejection.

Just when I'm about to die from humiliation, I feel his hands rest on my waist. I jump from the contact—his touch is warm. My breaths become laboured almost instantly. This is the first time he's really touched me like this, intimately. His hands lazily find their way up my back, his thumb stroking my spine. I curl into it. It feels wonderful.

He finds the zip at the top and slowly, too bloody slowly, pulls at it, all the way down to just above my arse. I don't dare turn around for fear of backing out.

His fingers divulge into the top and smooth over my bare shoulders underneath. God, the feeling of him on my skin is divine. The fabric falls down as his hands lower down, down, down until his hands are on the sides of my stomach. He must be able to feel me hyperventilating by now.

I look at myself half naked in the mirror and catch his eyes, alive with lust. Something inside me fires, setting my heart racing even faster. I quickly avert my eyes to the floor, unable to bear the raw sexiness of him.

His thumbs worm their way into the dress ruched at my hips. He tugs and it slips devastatingly slowly over my arse and drops in a bunch onto the floor. This is it. I'm standing in front of him in just my bra and knickers. Thank God I thought to put on nice stuff. Not that it's expensive. It's only Primark, but from here you could guess the pale pink satin was La Perla.

'You're beautiful,' he whispers in my ear, his voice like melting honey against my frayed senses. 'Even more so than I imagined.'

I feel myself blushing, desperate for his hands to be back on me.

'Look at yourself,' he whispers into my ear.

I look up into the mirror and find his eyes staring at me. The hunger in his eyes is palpable.

'You're fucking stunning.'

It feels all the more sexy because he's not touching me. My body hums with the need for his warm hands to feel me again, but this time, for them not to leave. His eyes are doing the work, taking in every minute detail of my body, as if he wants to memorise it forever. Every nerve ending in my body is begging him to close the distance.

'Champagne,' a voice sings from nowhere.

Hugh pushes me inside the changing room and pulls the curtain closed in an instant.

'Ah, thank you, Collette. I'll pass this on to the soon to be Mrs Humphrey.'

God, talk about knowing how to keep cool. He barely sounds flushed, while I'm still catching my breath.

'So it's true!' the squeaky voice says excitedly. 'It's

funny, but I always thought you'd end up marrying— '

'Collette!' he shouts quickly. 'Why don't you see if Martha needs any help, hmm?'

Wait, who the hell was she about to say? And why doesn't he want me to know?

He takes a few seconds before he pulls open the curtain holding two champagne glasses.

'For you, madam.'

I take it gratefully and knock back two gulps. I need the Dutch courage to ask him about this woman Collette saw him marrying. I open my mouth to ask when Martha appears.

'Right! I have some dress choices here which I think will look fabulous on those curves of yours.'

Curves? Is that her polite way of calling me fat? I wouldn't mind, but I'm really not that curvy. I'm an average size twelve. Most friends of mine have said they'd love to have my body.

'So, if you'd excuse us a minute,' she says to Hugh with a smile. 'Take a seat and get ready to be wowed.'

The first dress she shows me is silver and full of encrusted diamonds. I smile back positively. Then I'm showed a bright red number. It's not really me. A bit too bold and in-your-face for my liking. But the third dress, my God, the third dress. It's impossible for my jaw not to hit the floor.

A long, champagne coloured dress—simple yet enchanting.

'I think this is the one,' she smiles back, opening it up so I can step into it.

She pulls the thin spaghetti straps up over my shoulders and within seconds unclips my bra and throws it to the floor.

'This dress doesn't call for a bra,' she smiles.

The sweetheart neckline shows enough of my chest to look sexy, but she's right, without the bra, it looks nothing but classy and elegant. It's fitted at the waist and then falls in thin pleats to the floor, the sides and back longer than the rest, meaning when I move it trails behind me like a wedding dress. Wow.

'This is definitely the one,' she smiles proudly. 'Now to show it to your fiancée.'

She opens the curtain and walks me out to Hugh sat on a chaise lounge reading something on his phone.

I clear my throat, and he looks up immediately. His eyes widen in wonder when he spots me, his eyes scanning me from head to toe.

'You look...' he blows out a breath, 'absolutely stunning.'

Martha smiles proudly. 'I'll leave you two alone for a moment to discuss it.'

I beam back at her, to show I appreciate it.

'So?' I murmur self-consciously, doing a little spin. 'Do you really like it?'

He stands up and stalks towards me, like a predator about to attack. Be still my thudding, thumping heart.

'I don't just like it,' he purrs, standing in front of me. He takes a spaghetti strap between his finger and thumb. 'I love it.' He slips the strap down off my shoulder and moves onto the other side. 'In fact, I love it so much.' The next strap is pulled down painfully slowly. 'That I want to see what it looks like on the floor.'

I stare up at him with what I imagine is wanton lust. He spins me around and slowly undoes the zip. He yanks it off my shoulders in the middle of the room, my breasts exposed to anyone that might walk in.

His hands find them from behind, pawing at them greedily. Oh my God, he is beyond hot. He pushes me to the entrance of the changing room but stops without closing the curtain. I look at myself standing half naked in the mirror, my chest puffing up and down with need.

He slips his hand around to the front of my knickers. His fingers dip inside while the other hand yanks them down so roughly I have to use my hands to steady myself on the changing room doorframe.

He plays with my folds. I'm embarrassingly wet, so much so that one finger glides inside me without any effort. I gasp, clenching around it. The combination of the sensation and watching it happen in the mirror is so overwhelming that I can barely stand. He uses his other arm to wrap around my waist to steady me.

He circles his finger inside me, curling it up in just the right spot.

I groan loudly. God, did that sound really just come out

of my mouth?

'Shhh,' he hisses in my ear. 'We don't want Martha walking in.'

'Then close the curtain,' I hiss impatiently.

He pushes another finger in. 'But where's the fun in that?' I see his grin in the mirror at the same time as his thumb starts rubbing my clit in soft circles.

Oh my god. Control slips away from me. I don't care if Martha catches us. I'll do anything for him not to stop right now.

My head falls back onto his broad chest. I instinctively push my bum back into him and feel the hardness against his trousers. God, I want him. No, if he keeps moving his fingers like he is now, I fucking *need* him.

'I know we said we'd wait,' he whispers in my ear.

'Please,' I hiss back, unable to form a coherent sentence. 'Do it.'

Without missing a beat, he bends me over, and his belt buckle hits the floor with a clink. I peek a look at myself in the mirror, bent over, totally at his mercy. It's so hot.

He thrusts into me so roughly I fly forward and almost hit the mirror with my head.

'Shit,' I gasp. He's fucking huge!

I steady myself with my hands outstretched onto the mirror. He holds my hips in place forcing me to take all of him. Fuck, I think he just touched my womb.

He thrusts relentlessly into me, the feeling so full I want

78

to scream each time. It's so overwhelming a part of me wants to ask him to stop. But an even bigger part of me is begging me to take it, revel in it. Wait for the explosion of pleasure to hit me.

Tingling travels up my spine, my toes are curling so much I almost collapse as a feeling of total ecstasy takes over me, unleashing an exploding light, blinding me temporarily.

When I come back down to earth and open my eyes, I realise that his hand is over my mouth. A glance in the mirror tells me I must have been screaming. He locks eyes with me as his thrusts speed up until he tenses—squeezing my hip so hard I'm sure it'll bruise.

He collapses down onto the floor, taking me down with him.

'Fuck,' he groans, pulling me into his chest. 'That was amazing.'

I open my mouth to talk when I hear footsteps.

'Oops!'

I look up to see Martha standing over us, her little face contorted in shock.

I quickly try to cover myself up.

'What did I tell you?' she grins proudly. 'That dress is *definitely* the one.'

Chapter 8

'No way!' Nadine shrieks. 'You did *not* get caught having sex! Florence Gray! Do I even know you anymore?!'

'Ssssh!' I hiss, as we walk into the bridal store. 'I'm embarrassed enough!'

'And you should be,' she giggles, attempting to cover her mouth to try and stop them becoming cackles. 'You bloody harlot!'

'Who's a harlot?' Joan asks, looking between us with alarmed eyes.

'No-one!' I shout far too quickly. 'Anyway, let's get down to trying on dresses.'

'I'm so excited!' Mum coos, stroking me on the arm. 'I can't believe my baby girl is getting married. It seems like only yesterday you were in nappies.'

I smile, but lean back and whisper into Nadine's ear, 'Don't let her talk at the wedding.'

'Already on it,' she whispers back.

Nadine takes control and lets the shop owners know we're here. We're led into a separate little room and poured champagne. How swanky.

'So,' the gay Italian asks me. 'What kind of dresses are you looking for?'

'The cheapest,' I admit quickly.

Four horrified faces look back at me.

'What?' I argue defensively. 'Sorry, but I have a tight budget. And I need an even quicker turnaround. I'm getting married on Christmas day.'

'THIS Christmas day?' he repeats, hand on his chest as if I'm insane.

'Err...yeah. Why?'

His olive skin turns flushed. He fans himself with his hand.

'We normally advise brides to order their dresses six months ahead. Oh, my, my, my, my, my.'

God, he's a diva.

'You must have *something* I can wear in time.'

'Darling,' he says, clicking his fingers, his face contorted in horror, 'this is your wedding dress. It's not just *something* you drag out of a wardrobe. This is *zee* dress. It has to be *zee* dress of the century!'

'Besides, sweetheart,' Mum says with a sweet smile, 'this dress is going to be my treat.'

Great. Mum getting herself into debt. That's another thing to worry about.

'Mum,' I warn. 'I don't want you getting into debt just because of a stupid dress.'

The Italian's eyebrows nearly hit the ceiling. 'Stupid dress? Have you not heard a thing I've been saying?'

'I'm sorry, but he's right,' Nadine says sternly. 'I will not allow you to get some shitty dress just because it's cheap.'

'Finally!' he cries dramatically, flapping his arms up in the air. 'People talking sense.'

'Besides, sweetheart,' Mum reasons, 'I've been saving. This won't be going onto a credit card.'

No matter how annoying I find Joan at least she's finally offered my Mum financial stability.

I sigh. 'Okay, bring me the dresses.'

~

By the time he arrives back into the room nearly thirty minutes have passed. He may have left us with an extra two bottles of champagne, and we may be a little squiffy. Okay, a little shit-faced.

'Because of zee time problem we're going to have to choose a dress we already have in stock. Now, I don't want to scare you, but that means we have only two dresses.'

Mum and Nadine take a deep inhale of horrified breath. I roll my eyes. What bloody drama queens.

'That's fine,' I smile. 'I'm sure one of them will be nice.'

'Nice,' Nadine snorts sarcastically. 'Yeah, that's exactly what you want your wedding dress to be. *Nice.*'

'Let's see them,' I demand, choosing to ignore her.

He unzips the first bag and pulls out the most enormous ivory princess dress. I screw my face up. There are so many diamantes on that thing it's basically a very large disco ball. Who on earth would want to wear that?

'You like?' he asks, eagerly nodding his head like the Churchill dog.

'No,' I comment blankly. I can't help but hide the distaste on my face.

'Okay. We still have one.' He fetches the other bag and unzips it.

It's even worse than the previous. The shape isn't so bad, more of a classic type, but it's a weird kind of cream colour, almost like a yellow and it's got big navy parts all over the chest.

'You like?'

Am I being dramatic? I look to Mum, Joan and Nadine. They look gutted for me. Actually gutted. And the worst thing is that I feel crestfallen. I feel heartbroken. It seems I was holding out on this dress being beautiful a lot more than I realised. But these? I wouldn't be seen dead in them.

'Maybe try one on?' he suggests. 'Sometimes they look better on.'

I nod, unable to talk, a fresh bout of emotions tightening around my neck.

Nadine helps me get stripped down to my underwear,

and then I step into the disco ball dress. Fabio, or whatever his bloody name is, helps pull it up and starts tying the corset back.

It weighs a bloody tonne, and when I look back at myself in the mirror, I can't help but feel disappointed. This isn't me. This is more gypsy bride than anything.

'Well?' he asks hopefully, puffing out the edges, so they fall perfectly on the floor.

'I...' I literally cannot speak. Can't put into words the squashed feeling in my chest.

'She hates it,' Nadine says bluntly.

'Maybe move around in it, darling?' Mum offers with a grimace. 'You might get used to it.'

I step down from the small pedestal and attempt to walk towards the mirrors, but it's hard with the dress being so heavy. It's already hurting my back. I accidentally step on the skirt fabric and before I know it I'm falling, an almighty rip coursing through the air. I scrape my knee against the carpet. Fuck, that stings.

I lift myself up and look down at my legs. Arrgh, I have carpet burns so bad one of them is bleeding. Fuck my life.

'You ripped the dress!' Fabio shouts in horror.

Joan lifts up the dress to check my legs. 'She's bleeding!' she shouts dramatically. 'Somebody get a first aid kit!'

'Don't bleed on the dress! Don't bleed on the dress!' Fabio screams hysterically.

'Get me out of this!' I shout, suddenly feeling

suffocated. 'It's so tight I can barely breathe.'

'Get her out of the dress!' Nadine roars.

'You've ripped the dress!' Fabio complains. 'You have to pay for this.'

'We're not paying for a ripped dress,' Mum squawks with hand on her hip.

'A dress you ripped!!' he roars, throwing his hands in the air in exasperation.

'Help me,' I whimper, tears falling down my cheeks. The dress is so tight it's hurting to take breaths now, and it's like someone's turned the heat up to 100.

'Fuck it,' Nadine sighs behind me, grabbing her bag. She pulls out tiny nail scissors and starts hacking away at the corset strings. 'You're gonna be made to pay for it now anyway.'

Slowly my breath comes back to me. It lets me draw in enough breath to collapse into a pitiful crying mess.

If this is the start of things to come, do I really want to do this?

~

Friday 9th December

I can't believe we've had to shell out five hundred and fifty quid for a dress I don't even like. What a bloody nightmare. Bloody being the word. My knee bled like an old lady on Warfarin.

This decreases our budget even more. I haven't had the

guts to tell Hugh. He'd probably realise what a disaster I am and dump me immediately.

Tonight's the engagement party, completely organised by his Mum. His Mum who's going to ask me if I've signed the prenuptial agreement. Part of me thinks I should just sign it. If it gets her to pay for the wedding and take the burden off us, it almost seems worth it. Plus, if she likes me a bit more it won't hurt. Would probably make my life easier for the next lifetime. God, I finally find a man who wants to marry me and he has a psychotic mother. Typical.

I stand in front of the floor-length mirror in Hugh's apartment and study my reflection. The dress really is stunning, and I'm confident that I've scrubbed up well. My makeup is done to perfection, a mix of smoky and gold eye shadow accentuating my brown eyes. I've gone for a subtle pale brown lip stain, so it doesn't all look too much. My hair has been tonged and combed through so it looks effortlessly wavy. I've clipped it to one side in an attempt to show off my slim shoulders.

'You look stunning,' Hugh says from the doorway, gazing at me adoringly.

Bloody hell, he doesn't look so bad himself in his dinner suit and dickey bow. Who knew a dickey bow could be so bloody sexy?

'You look good yourself,' I appreciate with a wry smile.

My cheeks heat with the memory of him deep inside me. I clench my legs together to stop myself getting carried away and look down towards my trusty black high heels. I slide my feet in, trying to think of cooling things.

'Tell me something I don't know,' he grins, suddenly behind me. He places his hands on my bottom and gives my cheeks a little squeeze.

'Cheeky,' I say with a giggle over my bare shoulder.

'Do you think we could be a bit late?' he whispers into my ear, nipping my lobe.

My God, he's so bloody sexy. Just the idea of having him inside me again causes my stomach to curl up and purr.

'What, and get your Mother to hate me even more?'

He groans. 'You do have a point.' He stands up straight as if having to shake himself out of it. 'Come on then, Cinderella, before the magic wears off.'

That's what I'm worried about.

We arrive just after 8.30pm and are ushered into the main room of the Wyonging hotel. Now this is more like it. Marble floors, high arched ceilings and the clinking of champagne glasses in the distance.

As soon as we're through the door, people are slapping Hugh on the back, congratulating him. He politely thanks them with a back slap or two back, but I can tell there's no genuine fondness so far. His eyes haven't creased like they do when he laughs with me.

People are cooing at me as if I'm some trophy wife to be admired. No one actually talks directly to me or asks me any questions. It's all directed to Hugh, but he still keeps his arm linked with mine.

'Darling!'

We both turn to see his Mother walking towards us with her arms outstretched as if she hasn't seen either of us for years. She throws herself at him in an over-the-top embrace, breaking our link. He looks apologetically over his shoulder at me.

'Mother,' he says curtly in greeting. 'And you, of course, remember Florence.'

She begrudgingly looks over at me. 'Of course.'

She leans in to kiss me on the cheek, her scent invading my nostrils. So, this is what pure evil smells like.

'Have you signed the prenup yet?' she whispers discreetly into my ear.

I look over to Hugh. He narrows his eyebrows quizzically, obviously not having heard.

'Not yet,' I answer honestly with a grimace. 'But I hardly think it's something to discuss right now.' At my bloody engagement party, you horrible bitch.

'You're right,' she says with a fake smile. 'You should be mingling.'

I look around. There's not a single person I recognise.

'I will as soon as I find someone I know.'

Hugh's caught in conversation with a man in his fifties now. He looks bored to tears.

'Let me take you to your people then,' she says with a

snide smile.

I allow her to guide me away, smiling at Hugh. She steers me through the room, all the way out into the garden grounds. Shit, is she planning on killing me?

It's then I hear Kelly's laugh through the frostbitten night air.

'There they are,' she says, pointing towards a bench with my girls, Mum and Joan sat at it laughing their heads off.

Now, this looks like a party.

'Thanks,' I say through gritted teeth.

She's probably just glad to get me out of the way. Have her little Hugh all to herself.

'Look who it is!' Mia says when she spots me. 'The bride to be!'

They all laugh and whoop. Shit, how much booze have they already had? I spot four empty bottles of champagne on the table. When I get closer, I see that they're playing Cards Against Humanity. This could only end in disaster!

'Mum! You're not honestly playing this game, are you?' I ask with concern. For a lesbian, she sure gets offended easily, and this is not the game for people like that.

'I am, sweetheart,' she says with a hiccup. 'It's actually quite entertaining.'

'I think it's awful!' Joan says with distaste.

We all burst out laughing.

'Come on,' Kelly laughs, grabbing my hands. 'Let's get shit-faced.'

'I think you're already there,' Mia retorts with a snort.

'Well, it's not every day our bestie gets engaged!'

'How come you guys are out here anyway?' I ask as a shiver runs down my back.

They all look to Nadine. She sighs. 'Okay, the truth is that we didn't want to be around those stuck up old people. I mean, do you even know any of them?'

I roll my eyes. 'The only people I know are you guys.'

Sympathetic eyes settle on me.

'It's fine, though,' I quickly add dismissively. 'Kelly's right. Let's get drunk!'

~

By half eleven everyone is completely shit-faced, but even though I've sunk quite a few I can't seem to get there. I can't dismiss the unsettling feeling of melancholy that settles on me whenever I think of Hugh in there laughing with all of those pompous people. Is this what my married life is going to be like? Us living separate lives?

Maybe that's why he wants me. So, that he can carry on with his life and just rely on someone to look pretty and shag every now and again. I'm not on board with that. I want a partner that treats me like an equal. Not some trophy wife bimbo.

I say goodbye to everyone as they run off to get an Uber. Mia hangs back though.

'You okay, babe?' I ask her.

'Yeah,' she nods, her eyes sympathetic, 'but are you?'

I plaster on a fake smile. 'What do you mean?'

Just because I'm upset doesn't mean I want everyone worried about me. That'll just add to the stress.

'I mean, aren't you worried that you just spent your entire engagement party outside with us instead of with your fiancée?'

'Mia!' Nadine calls from the taxi. 'Hurry up!'

She smiles kindly at me before turning and running to catch up with them.

She's right. Of course, I know she's right. This whole thing is a sham.

I rub my arms, the cold night air seeping into my bones now I don't have Mum's poncho to keep me warm. I wander back into the reception room to find only a few stragglers remaining. My first reaction should be to find Hugh, but I find myself turning and walking into another empty room at the end and sitting in front of the open fire. Now that the warm flames lick at my body I realise how cold I've been outside. My body's like ice. I stare despondently at the blue and orange flames.

'Here you are.'

I turn my head to see Hugh sighing with relief, running his hand through his hair. 'Thank God. I've been looking for you everywhere.'

'Really?' I ask vaguely, staring back at the fire. He can't have looked that far, or he'd have found me.

'Yeah. Where the hell have you been? I've been stuck chatting to every boring bastard going while trying to find you and escape early.'

Likely story. It's not like he's going to admit he was having a whale of a time and barely noticed I'd gone until the party ended.

'I was only outside.' I'm glad I'm not looking at him so he can't see the hurt pouring from my every pore.

His footsteps walk closer. 'Outside? What the hell were you doing outside?' He kneels behind me and wraps his arms around my waist.

If I weren't so cold I'd shrug him off; let him know just how pissed off I am. But his body is warm and toasty, and mine can't help but gravitate towards it.

'Shit, you're freezing,' he gasps. He takes his jacket off and lays it over my shoulders.

My mood melts slightly at the warm gesture.

'I was outside with my Mum and friends. You know,' I add bitchily, 'people I actually know.'

He sighs, his body sagging against mine. 'I know exactly what you mean. My mother must have invited every single person she's ever met, yet my Grandma couldn't come.'

I turn to face him. He looks weary. Frown lines are etched into his forehead that weren't there at the beginning of the night.

'Tell me married life isn't going to be like this?'

He touches my chin and stares deeply into my eyes. 'I

promise with all of my heart that life with me will be nothing like this.' He places a soft kiss on my lips.

That's exactly what I needed to hear.

'It's made me decide something anyway,' I admit, wondering how he's going to react to my decision. 'I'm sorry, but I'd much rather get married in that shit hole of a pub with people I know and love, than have some circus and feel like a trophy wife paraded in to be looked at and not spoken to.'

He smiles, his eyes looking deep into mine. 'You want to get married in the pub?'

I smile back with a nod. 'I'm happy with that. I've never needed a big wedding.'

He tucks a stray bit of hair behind my ear. 'That's one of the things I'm learning to love about you. You don't give a shit about what people think. You care about the real things. And that's exactly what our marriage will be. Real.'

With words like that soothing over my frayed nerves it's easy to melt into the moment, the heat of the fire on my face, his body heat on my back. I just hope they're not just words.

Chapter 9

Saturday 10th December

'So these are your hand-held scanners. Feel free to wander round and 'zap' whatever you fancy.'

Hugh and I share excited faces. We decided to spend today getting registered at John Lewis. Finally, a fun wedding activity.

I put my scanner to his face, like a gun. 'You better stay on the right side of me. Whatever I want gets scanned, okay?' I joke, creasing up in laughter.

He grabs my hand and starts dragging me along behind him. 'Come on, let's head to the TV's.'

Is he serious?

'No way! You seriously think someone is going to spend that much on us?' I ask unconvinced.

'Who knows,' he grins mischievously. 'But it's worth a cheeky scan, right?'

We get to the TV area, and he's instantly cooing about all of the technology, rambling on about HD, 3D, Smart

TV. It's all like another language to me. I couldn't care less.

'Yeah, just get whatever you want,' I agree dismissively.

He goes to scan a 65" TV. Apart from that monster!

'Woah! You don't seriously think that will fit in our new house, do you?' I ask, blinking rapidly.

He narrows his eyebrows at me. 'You mean, the new house that we haven't bought yet?'

'Yeah, but it's not going to be a mansion, is it? Especially if we want to stay within a commute to London.'

It definitely won't fit that monstrosity in it. Why the hell would anyone want to watch a TV that big?

'So we'll just buy a house around the TV,' he shrugs with a smile.

Is he serious? I hope to God not.

'Why don't we move on to homewares,' I suggest. 'Something a bit more fun.'

He rolls his eyes. Clearly, the thought of throw cushions repulses him. Weirdo. But, ever the team player, he wanders with me over to the plates.

As I look down at them, I realise I have no idea what style we plan to decorate the new place. The new place we haven't even chosen yet. Maybe I'll get an idea from his choice of plates.

'What kind of plates do you like?' I ask, attempting to sound as easy going as possible.

He looks over them quickly. Too quickly for my

liking. Doesn't he realise what he's about to tell me may make or break our future harmony together?

'These are nice.' He picks up a square slate plate. Modern, edgy. Totally not my style. Dammit. Maybe if I suggest something I like, he'll see that they're an option too.

'Aren't these adorable,' I ask hopefully, holding up the most gorgeous plate. It's white in the centre with duck egg blue and yellow edging—vintage red roses splashed across them. It's vibrant but graceful. Vintage, but still modern. Plus, *so* adorable.

'Yeah,' he snorts. 'If you're an eighty-five-year-old.'

My mouth pops open in shock. 'Are you serious?'

How can he offend these beautiful plates? What is wrong with the man?

'Are *you?*' he asks in disbelief. 'Did you honestly expect me to like that? It's too fucking girly.'

I force myself to look at the plate from his perspective. I suppose it is kind of feminine. Doesn't stop me wanting it though. Maybe we can get it and only take it out when my friends come over. They'd bloody love it. Plus, the set has a matching cake stand.

'This is pointless anyway,' he announces with a sigh. 'Before we know what kind of kitchen we have, we won't know what we want. We should be house viewing today instead.'

I slump, feeling defeated. I just wanted to do something

fun. The truth is, I really don't want to leave my flat, but I suppose I need to grow up and move on. God, just the thought of living with a guy is giving me hives. What if he leaves his dirty socks on the floor? What if he shaves in the sink and doesn't clean up after himself?

'Hugh?' a woman's voice calls, breaking me from my horrifying thoughts.

We both turn, plates in hands, to face a tall red head with glossy Victorian ringlet curls. She's got pale porcelain skin with not one single blemish on it and piercing blue eyes. She could be a model. Who the hell is this?

'Felicity,' he gasps, his face paling. 'What are you doing here?'

She grins. 'Shopping, obviously,' she giggles.

Oh my god. This is Felicity; the ex girlfriend. The girlfriend his Mum wanted him to marry. No wonder Hugh's looking so freaked.

'What about you?' she enquires, looking at me with interest.

He shakes his head as if trying to clear his mind. 'This is my fiancée, Florence.' He takes my elbow and pulls me over to him before wrapping his arm protectively around me.

'Ah,' she nods. 'I never got to meet you last night.'

She attended my engagement party? Hugh's ex-girlfriend? I look to Hugh, and then back at her.

'You were there last night? At our engagement party?'

97

'More than you, it seems.' She throws back her head in a totally ridiculous over the top posh laugh. Imagine a horse having a panic attack, and you're almost there. 'Poor Hugh here was very fraught, looking for you.'

I look back at him. He's fidgeting from foot to foot, looking as if he'd rather be anywhere but here right now.

'Nice to finally meet you,' she says extending her perfectly French manicured hand for me to shake. I take it, but she grips so tight, shaking so hard I'm worried she'll rip my arm out of the socket. Jesus, where did she learn to shake hands? The military?

'You two used to go out, right?' I ask, glad I know enough to ask.

Hugh's cheeks turn pink. She looks coyly to the floor.

'Yes,' Hugh admits awkwardly. 'But we're still friends.'

He's friends with an ex of his? An ex that is THIS good looking? And from her voice, she's clearly posh just like him and his family. His Mother basically said she'd rather he marry someone like her. And if they're so bloody friendly, why didn't he just ask her to marry him?

'So...you broke up a long time ago?' I enquire, attempting to sound casual.

Hugh's grip on my waist tightens.

'Oh, completely!' she giggles. 'Golly, it must be at least six months ago now!'

Six months? Six fucking months? That's no time at all!

I turn to look at Hugh in disbelief, expecting some kind

of explanation.

'All in the past now,' he agrees hurriedly.

'So how long have you been together then?' she asks me with an eager grin. 'Hugh here was a bit vague when I asked him.'

Oh, Shit. I can't exactly tell her the truth, can I? She'll think I'm insane. She'll think Hugh's insane too.

'Not too long,' I smile, not wanting to give anything away.

Hugh hugs me tighter, obviously pleased with my answer.

'Really? How long exactly?' she presses. 'It can't be more than five months, can it?'

'Um...' Hugh babbles, pouting as if trying to work out the time. 'Bit shorter than that I think.'

'It's been such a whirlwind romance,' I admit, choosing to stroke his hair back.

We all know it's an act of dominance. If I were a dog, I'd be pissing on him right now. He's claimed, bitch, back off.

'You must have swept him off his feet,' she agrees, smiling smugly. 'When we were together the idea of marriage horrified him.'

'Really?'

'I wouldn't say horrified,' he argues, awkwardly.

'Were you together long then?' I ask, unable to hide my curiosity. I get the feeling I'll find out more from her than I ever will from him.

She nods. 'Three years.'

I nearly choke on air. Three years? He was with her three years, and he didn't want to marry her? Now he's known me a few days and is supposedly sure. What the hell is wrong with the guy? Does he have some kind of hidden mental health problems?

'Anyway,' Hugh interrupts, 'sorry, Flic, but we must get on.' He calls her Flic? That irks me much more than it should. 'We're registering.'

'Ooh, how exciting!' She walks over and picks up the same plate Hugh had suggested. 'I've had my eye on these plates for a while. Anyway, see you soon!'

Shit. She's made for him. She wants his plate. She wants the same things he wants. She's from the same background. Why the hell didn't it work out? Am I just a ploy to get her back? Show her that he's ready to commit now?

'Will we see her soon?' I question, eyeing him suspiciously. 'Are you seriously still friends with her? You can't be that close if she doesn't know how long we've been together.'

He avoids my eye line, choosing instead to look over more plates. 'Please, we're barely even friends. I just had to say that to be polite.'

'So, why will we see her soon?'

'Ugh,' he rolls his eyes with a loud sigh. 'Her Mum is best friends with my Mum. She's bound to be invited to the wedding.'

'*Our* wedding?' I repeat, eyes wide. 'Sorry, I was under the illusion that we'd be sticking with our original guest list seen as she's no longer paying?'

'You don't get it though,' he says with a grimace. 'I couldn't be seen to not invite them. I've known them all my life.'

'Yet you still forgot to add them to the original list.'

He pulls me close to him. 'I'm sorry. It doesn't bother you, does it?'

I wrap my hands around his neck. 'Your ex-girlfriend attending our wedding?'

'She's an ex for a reason you know,' he smiles, pecking a kiss on my nose.

'Why did you break up?'

'Because she wanted to get married.'

I pull away from him. 'And now you're showing her that you're up for getting married.' This is just as I thought. He's using me. 'Be honest with me, Hugh, am I just a ploy to make her jealous so you can end up with her? Because you can't play games like that with me.'

'No! Jesus, I'd never do that. I didn't want to marry her because she's a high-maintenance fucking princess. You're the complete opposite of her.'

'And that's enough?'

I mean, her hair was perfect. Bitch.

'You are more than enough,' he smiles, pecking me

lightly on the lips. 'I can't wait to spend the rest of my life getting to know you.'

'And what if I turn out to be a princess?'

He grins. 'You're already my princess.'

I snort. 'You're beyond cheesy. If anything, I'm a Goddamn queen.'

'As long as you're my queen I don't care how demanding you get. Especially in the bedroom.'

Okay, he's mine. I just have to make sure Felicity knows that.

~

Hugh's gone off to check on a building or something. I really need to start listening when he talks about work, but the minute he's talking about building codes I can't help but zone out. Anyway, I'm doing wedding stuff. AGAIN. I'm actually glad we've condensed the stress into twenty-four days. I don't think I could handle it spread out over a year, like a normal person.

Anyway, today I'm seeing a photographer's wedding portfolio, and I'm bloody excited! His website is amazing, and I think if I turn on my charm we might even be able to get what we want within our budget.

I'm a bit early to meet Nadine here, but I'm too eager to see what his studio looks like inside. I open the large oak door and attempt to take in the cool, edgy surroundings.

Its walls are painted a dark blue, black and white

photographs hanging from almost every spare wall. I look towards what seems like a main stage. A photographer is taking pictures of a woman and her child. Wow, that kid's got a big honker. I hope the photographer is good with Photoshop.

'Um...hi,' I mumble awkwardly, 'I'm— '

'You're late,' he snaps at me, his gaze hard. 'We have to be quick.'

Wow. He's rude.

'Sorry, what?'

But he's already pushing me off to the side of the room. I open my mouth to speak again, but he's pushing me behind a room divider. What the hell is going on here?

'If you strip down, I'll just fetch your outfit.'

'But, I—' It's too late—he's already walked away.

Well, I know about photographers being divas. Hell, I deal with them on a day-to-day basis, but this is just taking the piss. And why does he want me to get changed into an outfit? Maybe he wants to do some test shots of me in a bridal dress? I suppose that could make sense. And I do understand that some of the most brilliant minds have questionable methods. Who am I to argue?

'Let's hurry it up, please,' he yells over. 'I have another appointment in ten.'

Shit, he's bossy.

I quickly pull my jeans and top off, throwing them over the divider.

'I want you on set in two,' he shouts, throwing something back over.

I take it off and look at it. What the hell is this? A black and red Basque with matching French knickers?

'Excuse me,' I shout over. 'Excuse me!'

There's no reply. I peek around it to see he's nowhere to be seen. Shit. What the hell am I going to do? He's taken my normal clothes. If I plan on confronting him, I'm going to have to put on this ridiculous slutty outfit.

I begrudgingly wiggle into it, of course over my current bra and knickers. It's easily a size too small for me. My boobs are bursting over the top, but I'll have to make it work. It's still better than confronting him naked.

I check both ways to make sure no one else is around before running out quickly. I find him setting up his camera in front of a chaise lounge. Right, time to confront him.

'Sorry, but this is— '

'Ah, you're here!' he says over me. He grabs my arm and places me down on the chaise lounge. 'Now, look seductive.'

Seductive? Is he crazy? Does realise that I'm clearly not a lingerie model? He can't be paying that much attention to detail if he hasn't noticed my bra underneath the sexy Basque.

'Look, I really don't see how this is going to help me,' I insist. 'I'm just here for—'

'Just pout and think of England,' he interrupts, already snapping away.

'I beg your pardon!' I shout, horrified. 'I don't see how this is helping me choose you as a photographer.'

'Oh yeah, just there, love,' he calls enthusiastically. 'You looked really pissed off. It was hot.'

'But—'

'Come on, love,' he snaps impatiently, 'I need to get this done quick. I've got a bride to be coming to view my portfolio any minute.'

'Actually...'

Nadine's suddenly behind him, mouth agape.

'Florence! What the fuck is going on here?'

The photographer looks between us. 'You two know each other?'

'I'm...kind of...the bride to be,' I admit with a grimace.

~

Saturday 10th Dec

'I still can't believe you actually stripped off!' Nadine laughs, clutching at her sides.

'He was pushy!' I protest with a cringe. 'Plus, he left me with nothing else to wear!'

'Yeah, but getting changed into that Basque! It'll forever be imprinted in my mind.' She fakes a shudder.

'It's not my fault he'd booked in a boudoir shoot just before me, is it? Just stop talking about it!' I beg on a whine. 'Every time I think about it I feel like someone's set me on fire with humiliation.'

My phone buzzes in my bag. I reach into it and smile when I see it's Hugh. It's strange how already he's managed to worm his way into my heart.

'You've really got it bad,' she comments with a grin. 'Go ahead, answer to your *fiancée.*'

'Hi,' I say, shyly down the phone, fiddling self-consciously with my hair.

'Hey, sexy,' he practically purrs down the line. 'How was the photographer?'

'Err...I'm not sure if we'll be booking him. Kind of a long story.' That I never intend to tell you.

'Oh, okay,' he says, surprised. 'Anyway, are you free? I wanted to show you something.'

'Oh yeah,' I grin. 'I bet you do, big boy.'

Nadine pulls a face and pretends to hang herself.

He chuckles down the line. 'No, not that. Well, not yet anyway. Can you meet me at the pub we're gonna book?'

I sigh. Just thinking about that place makes me feel low.

'Oh, that beautiful place. I'll rush right over,' I laugh, sarcastically.

He chuckles. God, just the delicious sound of it makes me want to crawl inside the phone and dry hump him.

'I have a surprise for you.'

I look down at my glass of Prosecco, suddenly eager to down it.

'I'll just finish my drink with Nadine and head over.'

'Okay, see you soon.'

~

By the time I get there its seven pm and already pitch black outside. It's creepy around here. The pub is in the middle of the countryside, and there's only one streetlight letting off the slightest amber glow. I try to call him, but it just rings off to answerphone. Damn it.

I begrudgingly step out of the car and slam it behind me.

'BOO!' Hugh shouts, leaping out in front of me.

I jump out of my skin, my nerves completely shattered. 'N-n-not funny!' I stammer. My mouth is chattering from both the cold and crippling fear still coursing through me.

'Sorry, but it was too easy.'

He grabs the collar of my coat and pulls me in for a kiss, his warm lips begging me to forgive him. I let myself melt into him as he kisses me slowly and deeply, his cold hands on my face. It quickly turns into a deep passionate kiss, his warm tongue caressing mine. I groan into it.

He reluctantly pulls back. 'Right, now for your surprise.'

I frown. What the hell could he be surprising me with here? I'd be happy for a quick shag in the car.

He walks towards the door but instead of going in he leads me around the back.

'Where are we going?' I ask, mystified.

He smiles broadly. 'You'll see.'

When we get to the garden, that I didn't even know existed, I see that it's lit up with fairy lights.

Out jump Mia, Kelly, Troy, Jace, and Nadine. 'Surprise!'

I turn to Hugh in confusion. 'What's going on?'

He smiles at me, rubbing my knuckles with his thumb. 'We're going to show you how our day can still be amazing.'

'Yeah,' Nadine agrees, rushing forward. 'Imagine all of this garden lit up with fairy lights.'

'And wait until you see inside,' Kelly gushes, her cheeks pink with the cold. 'It's gorgeous.'

Troy agrees with a nod. 'We've all said we'll help decorate it and bring it up to scratch.'

'It'll be cool,' Mia nods, with a wink. 'Just wait and see.'

Bless them. All coming out and doing this, just to try and please me. What are they like? I can't help but feel all Christmassy, surrounded by so much love.

'Come on,' Hugh says, guiding me towards the inside of what looks like a barn.

The moment the doors open I'm met with candlelight. Tea lights are on every table and church candles on every other available surface, emitting such a soft glow that the ugliness is faded into the background—instead it looks pretty and romantic.

Hugh takes my hands and looks deep into my

eyes. 'Trust me when I say that if this is the place we have to get married, then I won't sleep until it's as good as it can be.'

'How have I ended up with someone so sweet?'

And can shag like a jackhammer.

'You're just a lucky girl,' he winks, slapping me on my arse. 'Now let's go back to yours so I can bend you over and fuck you raw.'

Jesus, someone pinch me! It seems I've been a very good girl and Santa has brought my present early.

Chapter 10

Tuesday 13th December

So, Hugh is eager for me to meet his Grandma Clara. Apparently, they're really close. Well, closer than him and his mother anyway, which I suppose isn't hard. He's taking us to meet at Winter Wonderland and has booked for us to go ice-skating. She must be bloody nimble if she's able to ice skate. Hugh says she's only seventy-five, but that's still old in my book.

As we walk through the entrance of Hyde Park, I can't help but feel ecstatic. I come here every year. I love the smell of German sausage and mulled wine. Even though it's only one pm, there are low-lying grey clouds making it dark enough to make out the glow from the twinkle lights hung all around. It's bloody magical.

'You're in your element here, aren't you?' he asks, cocking up an amused eyebrow.

'A little bit,' I admit with a wide grin.

I can't help it! Christmas has always been such a

magical time for me. It didn't matter how poor we were when we were growing up, Mum always made sure that we celebrated. We went to every free event, even if we had to take a packed lunch and weren't allowed to buy anything.

I remember one Christmas, mum worked extra hard just so that she could afford for me to meet Father Christmas. Well, the one they put on in the shopping centre near us. I remember how he told me to 'follow my dreams'. Those words were so influential on the person I've now become.

Whenever I got down and thought I'd end up like my mum, skint and struggling, I'd remember that Father Christmas had faith in me. It helped me work harder. And let me tell you, working your way up as a makeup artist is not for the faint-hearted. Not that I believed in him all the way through my twenties. But...well...I was one of the last to find out.

Hugh smiles at me affectionately. 'As long as you don't sit on Santa's knee and start professing that you're a ho ho ho.'

I gasp and smack him in the arm. 'Stop! There are kids around.'

He looks down at a little blonde boy giggling hysterically as his Dad tickles him.

'How many kids do you reckon we'll have?'

I stop walking from utter shock. Wow, change in direction or what?!

'I don't know. How many would you like?' I suppose we should be having these kinds of conversations. Most couples have it before getting engaged.

'I was an only child, so I'd like a whole bunch,' he says with a wistful smile.

'Whole bunch?' I repeat in horror. Shit, is he planning on me pushing out the Brady Bunch? 'Don't get me wrong, I was an only child too, but remember it's my vagina they're coming out of.'

He chuckles. 'And what a lovely vagina it is.'

A Mum overhears him, her eyes doubling in size. She covers her daughter's ears and turns to run in the opposite direction.

'Maybe two or three then,' Hugh says, clearly having missed the Mum's reaction. 'I can always pay for you to have vaginal reconstructive surgery.'

'Bahah!' I laugh, exploding into a fit of giggles. 'Do you think most people talk like this after only a few dates?'

He muses for a second. 'Probably not. But then I suppose most people wouldn't have got engaged after only one date.'

'Yep, we're a bit different, to say the least,' I chuckle. 'Is your Nan going to think the same thing?'

I can't help but worry what she's going to be like. What if she's just as judging as everyone else?

'That you'll need reconstructed vaginal surgery?' he jokes. 'I'm not sure.'

I dig him in the ribs, attempting to frown but only managing to smile. 'Shut up! You know what I mean.'

He chews his lip. 'I've told her we haven't been together long, but no, I haven't been specific.'

'Great,' I say under my breath. So, there will be a confrontation.

'And there she is.' I follow his eye line to find a tall, thin woman with brown hair set in tight curls around her face. She definitely doesn't look seventy-five. Shit, she barely looks sixty.

'*That's* your Nan?' I ask, needing the clarification.

'Yeah,' he beams. 'Come on.'

He tugs my hand towards her. She turns, spots us and starts waving.

'Grandma, this is the beautiful, Florence.'

Her eyes light up as she scans me from head to toe. 'And beautiful she is! Come here, my dear.'

She grabs me and throws me into a bear hug. Wow, she's friendly. And strong for such a thin thing. She feels so frail in my arms.

'Right, let's get to know each other, shall we?' she says cheerfully, pulling us over to collect our skates.

Before we know it, we're on the ice. I forgot to mention that I haven't skated in years, but it's just one of those things you remember, right? Like riding a bike.

'Try and keep up with me,' she sings with a wink.

Oh, bless her.

'I'll try,' I joke back.

But fuck me, she's off! I've never seen someone skate like it. She's so long and lithe as she sweeps through the ice. It almost looks like she's going to...yep she's doing a spin. A bloody spin!

'Her and my Grandfather used to skate a lot when they were younger,' Hugh explains.

'Yeah, no shit,' I laugh, barely managing to stay upright. Every time I attempt to move a foot the other one slides away from me.

She skids to a halt in front of me, spraying my face with ice. 'Isn't this fun.'

'Yeah,' I say stiffly, forcing a smile. 'If I could just stop falling over.'

'Oh, you'll be fine,' She says, dismissing my concerns. 'Hugh should teach you. His Grandfather was quite the wiz.' She winks cheekily. It reminds me of Hugh.

So, is this where he got his personality from? It would make more sense than his Mum and Dad.

'I like the idea of skating,' I admit. 'I grew up watching *By the Light of the Silvery Moon* every Christmas.'

Her eyes light up. 'I *love* that film! That was one of mine and Herald's favourite films. That and *It's a Wonderful Life.*'

'I love that one too!' Watching Christmas videos was one cheap thing we could afford to do. 'We should do a movie night.'

She looks to Hugh as he skates to a stop by us. 'She has great taste. I love her already.'

'Of course she does. She chose me, didn't she?' he grins, pecking a kiss on my forehead.

A little later when I've been released from the first aiders, we've given back our skates and are browsing round at one of the sweet stalls, she turns to me.

'Tell me, Florence, do you love my Grandson?' Her forehead furrows.

Woah. Don't hold back Granny.

I look over at Hugh on the phone. Do I love him? I mean, I've only known him 13 days, but yeah, I'm a bit crazy about him. What's not to love? But am I already madly, would die if something happened to him, in love with him? Not yet. Can I lie to an old lady?

'Um...I think I will,' I admit with a hopeful smile. 'I'm not sure what Hugh's told you, but this was a crazy idea we came up with on our first date.'

She smiles kindly. 'He didn't tell me, but the way he was avoiding questions I could have guessed something strange had happened. Thank you for not lying to me.'

Phew. That was obviously some kind of hidden test.

'I'm sorry. This whole idea is kind of mental, but I've somehow been swept away by it.'

'Are you having doubts?' she asks kindly, her eyes imploring me to trust her.

'I don't know,' I admit with a shrug of my shoulders. 'If I were dating Hugh I'd be mad about him, and don't get me wrong, I am. Its just...marriage is a big deal to me. I plan on only getting married once. If this doesn't work out, I'll be devastated, and I suppose I don't know if he's really in this for life. Or if he's thinking divorce can be a get-out clause. Especially now I've promised to look at signing the prenup.'

Her eyes widen to twice the size. 'He made you a prenuptial agreement?' Her nostrils flare. 'I thought I'd raised him better than that!'

'No! It was his Mum that asked me to sign it, and I mean, she's just looking out for him. If I had a son, I'd probably be just as protective.'

'Hmm,' she snorts. 'But I bet you'd deliver it a lot nicer. My daughter has no manners.'

I stare back at her in shock. 'She's *your* daughter?'

I just assumed with her being so lovely her son was Hugh's Dad. Not that monster of a Mother.

'I know,' she grins like she's in on the joke. 'I get that reaction a lot.' She stares off into the distance. 'She was such a shy girl when she was growing up and so well mannered. The minute she met Hugh's father and got some money behind her, she turned.'

I suppose I can see how money could change a person for the worst.

'We refused her money, so be prepared for a mediocre

wedding.'

She smiles sadly. 'Darling, the wedding is only a day. The marriage is for life. That's where the investment should be placed.'

Is it wrong that I'm doubting whether I love Hugh, but I'm already one hundred percent sure that I love his Grandma?

'I know, you're right.' I look back to Hugh, still chatting away on the phone. 'I just really hope he's all in too.'

'I think I'm going to buy some of this fudge,' she says cheerfully, completely off subject.

I look down at the mediocre fudge. 'My Mum used to make the best fudge when I was younger. Every Christmas she'd put heart shaped fudge wrapped in tissue paper in my stocking. I loved it.'

She smiles. 'Your Mother sounds lovely.'

A text pings through on my phone. I look down at the unknown number. Grandma's busy filling a paper bag with fudge, so I chance a quick look.

```
Florence, Felicity here.  I was hoping
we could meet for a coffee?  There are
some things you really need to know.
```

Fuck! What the hell does that mean?

'Good news,' Hugh beams, back with us. 'I've got us a few house viewings for later in the week.'

'Really?' I frown. We haven't even talked about an area, yet alone what we're looking for in a house. 'I haven't looked at anything yet.'

'You'll love them,' he promises confidently.

It irks me that he's assuming I'll like them. I'm not going to be some agreeable bimbo that he's been used to in the past.

'Maybe I should select a few too. Just in case.'

'Okay,' he nods, clearly surprised that I'm doubting him. 'I'll text you their details, but I'm telling you, you're gonna love the ones we're viewing.'

Hmm, don't hold it against me if I don't take your word for it.

I look down at the text message. I can't help it. I reply.

`Tomorrow at 1 pm.`

Chapter 11

I tap my finger nervously on the side of my coffee cup. I have no idea what I'm doing here. Going behind Hugh's back. Hugh who's done nothing but give me reasons to trust him. Well, apart from being on the phone all the time. I can't help but find that suspicious. Why does he feel the need to walk away when he answers if it's just business calls?

Either way, I know I won't be able to rest until I find out what this Felicity wants. Even if it is only to cause trouble. My stomach feels in knots at the possibilities.

I look up just in time to see her walk through, all red curls bouncing gloriously along. Damn it, she's beautiful. I can tell she doesn't even wear much makeup. She's an English rose. Bitch.

'Florence,' she smiles, taking me in an awkward hug.

'Hi, Felicity.' I sit down and watch while she confidently orders a mocha latte.

'So...' I start, wringing my hands on the table. 'You

wanted to meet today. What's up?'

She looks down at the table, her face growing troubled.

'It's a little awkward...and I don't want you to get the wrong idea and think I'm trying to cause trouble.'

Oh, here we go. Something someone says just before they try to cause said trouble.

'But? What?' I push, sounding pretty aggressive. I just want to hear her bullshit so that I can dismiss it.

'I wondered whether Hugh told you how we broke up?'

I can't tell her I know it's because he didn't want to marry her.

'He mentioned it briefly,' I say as vaguely as I can, looking down into my coffee.

Her mocha latte gets delivered, and she pauses to take a sip. Trying to build up the tension, drama queen bitch.

'We'd been together a good few years, and I was desperate to get married. He was never really into it.'

So far this is what I know.

'Anyway, I fell pregnant.'

Shit. Bombshell. KABOOM!

'It obviously wasn't planned,' she explains, with a sad smile, 'but Hugh promised to stand by me. He even proposed.'

I nearly choke on my coffee. Engaged?

'You were *engaged?*' I utter in disbelief.

Wow. This changes everything. He lied to me. He told me he never wanted to get married to her, and now I hear he proposed. Just like he proposed to me. It makes my proposal feel tainted. Does he just propose to everyone?

'Yes,' she nods, 'but only briefly. You see, I knew he'd only proposed because of the baby. No matter how I tried to think about it, it always came back to that fact. Without meaning to, I'd trapped him. It was the baby keeping him.'

I smile sadly back at her. I'm not sure what else to do. I can't help but feel terribly sorry for her.

'Anyway, around the ten-week mark I lost the baby.'

My mouth drops open.

'Oh my god. I'm so sorry.'

This is so not the story I was expecting to hear. Where's the bitch telling me he doesn't love me? This is genuinely heart wrenching.

'Yeah, it was awful. Hugh and I were understandably devastated, and in my grief, I pushed him away. I broke off our engagement and told him I didn't want him anymore. I just couldn't bear him staying with me out of pity.'

I'm really not sure where this story is going now. She looks like going to continue.

'He begged for me to take him back, but I told him he wasn't the marrying type. That he didn't have that kind of commitment in him.'

Now the pieces of the puzzle are starting to come together. She's insinuating that the only reason he got engaged to me was to prove to her he's the marrying type. Make her jealous so that she begs for him to come back to her.

'So, you think he wants you back?' I ask bluntly.

She fidgets in her lap. 'I'm not sure. The first I heard of it was the engagement party invitation.'

Okay, that's a good sign. It means he didn't go straight to her to tell her of the engagement. Plus, he didn't even send the invite.

'Look, don't worry. His Mother sent that invitation, not Hugh. I know what you're trying to say; that he's using me to make you jealous, but I seriously doubt that. What me and Hugh have is real.'

She frowns. 'Are you sure?'

'Trust me,' I smile smugly. 'You don't fuck like we do in order to make someone else jealous.'

Her face drops. Ha, that shut her up. Yeah, bitch. I've got your man, and he's not going anywhere. God, when did I get so ghetto?

I stand up and grab my bag. 'Now, thanks very much for your concern, but I know full well what I'm getting into, and so does Hugh.'

She opens her mouth to respond, but I don't give her the chance. I storm out of there, leaving her to pay the bill. I'm sure she has a bag full of dosh, the swarmy, posh bitch.

I walk out onto the high street, the cold air making my ears sting. That or someone's talking about me. How the fuck could this happen? I might have played it up to her, but the truth is that this is something that a fiancée should know. It's something that should have been shared during one of those deep and meaningful late night chats you have in the first year. But we've barely learnt each other's middle names, let alone discussed a previous pregnancy and engagement.

I have to speak to him. I need to know—need to hear from his own lips that I'm not a consolation prize. That I'm not some stupid ploy to win Felicity back. And my worst fear—that I'm not some handy baby-making machine that he needs in order to stop his grieving.

With every day that passes, I feel more and more unsure of this marriage. God, sometimes I just feel like I need some sort of sign that I'm doing the right thing. That everything will work out.

That's when I see it. Staring back at me from the window. My dress. My dream wedding dress that I didn't even know I wanted. It's like someone has gone into my head and worked out what would look perfect on me.

The fitted bodice is asymmetrically pleated and falls off the shoulder making a portrait neckline. It flares into a sculptured organza ball gown skirt with horsehair edged layers. It's so simple, yet bloody stunning. A nod to old Hollywood. I need it.

I wander into the shop, as if under a spell.

'The dress,' I stammer frantically, pointing at it. 'In the window.'

She frowns. 'I'm afraid we've been meaning to remove

that all day.'

'What?' Oh god. I feel my hope sinking like the Titanic.

'The supplier has discontinued the line, and we've just placed our last order. There's only this sample left.'

'What size is it?' I ask, secretly praying that it'll fit me.

She grimaces. 'It's a twelve. Do you think that would fit you?'

Hope inflates in my chest like a balloon.

'Is the Pope a Catholic? Let's try on that bad boy!'

~

My God, it's like the dress was designed especially for me. It fits like a glove and makes me look so much taller and elegant than I actually am. I have to have it, but I haven't dared ask the price. I don't want the last bit of reality to crash down around me.

'It was on special offer,' the lady says, fussing around with the dress. 'But because it's the last dress left...'

Oh God, she's going to double it in price. She knows I've fallen hook line and sinker for it and she's using it to her advantage. What a bitch. Just when I think this wedding might not be doomed, this happens.

'And because I can see you love it, I'm willing to give you a further twenty percent discount.'

I nearly pass out in shock.

'What? You're joking! How much? How much?'

She smiles sweetly. 'I'm not joking. Rarely do I see a

bride suit a dress so well.'

'I bet you say that to all the brides,' I laugh, slightly hysterical. I need that price. Need to hear it out loud. If I can't afford it, I think I'll scream and be admitted to a mental ward.

'With all the discounts it falls at £575.'

I know my heart should drop in my chest and I should realise defeat. It's over budget. But I don't. Instead, I'm handing over my credit card and thanking God such a dress was created. I just won't mention it to Hugh.

~

Thursday 15th December

Hugh's picking me up from mine for us to go house viewing. I finally found a place I liked on their website. It's the most adorable three-bed cottage with original doors, a butler sink and the cutest little garden.

He buzzes up. 'You ready?' he asks in a husky voice.

'Coming down.'

I practically skip towards his car to him waiting with my door open. I lean over to peck a quick kiss on his lips.

'What are you so chipper about?' he asks with a quizzical grin.

'Nothing,' I say with a secret smile.

He shuts the door and jumps in his side. 'Seriously. You're freaking me out. What's happened?'

'I found my dress,' I admit, unable to hide my

happiness.

'No way! I bet that's cheered you right up.'

'Yep. Just when I was having doubts, I got the sign I needed.'

He frowns. 'Just when you were having doubts?'

Uh-oh. I didn't want to let him know that. Damn happiness taking over any rational thoughts.

'No, I didn't mean that.'

'You obviously did,' he counters, suddenly serious.

'No. It's just...' Oh God, I really don't want to ruin my good mood right now, and I know if I bring up Felicity it will be ruined. 'I was just freaking out earlier. I'm totally fine now.'

'You're sure?' he asks, furrowing his eyebrows at me.

'Positive,' I nod. 'Now let's see some houses!'

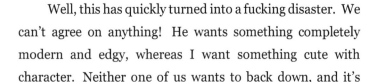

Well, this has quickly turned into a fucking disaster. We can't agree on anything! He wants something completely modern and edgy, whereas I want something cute with character. Neither one of us wants to back down, and it's going to end ugly.

We're just walking around the cottage bedroom of the house I picked when he says everything I've been thinking.

'We're never going to agree on anything, are we?'

'Not when you're so pig headed!' I bark, bad temperedly. 'What the hell is wrong with this place? It's adorable.'

'Yeah, for a midget! This bedroom won't even fit my king size bed in it.'

'It totally would!' I protest, hand on my hip. 'I don't want a modern, ugly Lego house!'

He runs his hands through his hair and sighs. 'Maybe we should just forget it.'

Oh my god. He's admitting it. We're not right for each other.

'Oh, that would work out for you, wouldn't it!' I snap, barging past him into the hallway. 'Show Felicity, how you're marriage material, and then just dump me. I'm just collateral damage to you, aren't I!'

He holds his hands up in defeat. 'Woah. What the fuck are you talking about?'

I barge past him again, back into the bedroom. I throw myself face down on the bed. Well, I've fucked it up now, haven't I?

I feel the bed sink lower as he lies down next to me. He places his hand on my shoulder and pushes me back, so I'm facing him.

'Why on earth would you say that?' he asks, his eyes looking deeply into mine, trying to figure out why I'm acting so hostile towards him.

Oh God, I'm going to have to admit it.

'I met up with Felicity for coffee.'

His eyes widen before such a huge frown appears on his

127

forehead, I'm sure he's going to have to start saving for Botox. 'You did? Why?'

'Because she asked me to.'

I can already see him closing down. It's like shutters are slamming down in his eyes. He knows I know the truth.

'And what did she tell you?' he asks with a gulp.

I have to tell him. I take a deep breath. 'She told me about the baby.'

His jaw tenses, his eyes closing as if I've slapped him. 'She had no fucking right,' he finally growls.

'She didn't do it to be a bitch,' I find myself admitting. 'She just wanted to warn me. She doesn't want me getting hurt.'

He scoffs. 'You don't get it. She dumped me. It wasn't enough our baby had died. Then she threw me to the side like I wasn't good enough for her.'

This doesn't sound like someone over his ex. This sounds like someone still hung up on her.

'So...if she hadn't have dumped you, would you still be together?'

He thinks for a moment before pushing his head into the bed. 'No. I was about to end it just before I found out about the baby. I would have broken up with her eventually, but unlike her, I wasn't heartless enough to do it straight away—while we were grieving.'

That actually makes me feel better.

'So you definitely don't want her back?'

'No,' he snaps. 'For fuck's sakes, this is what she wants. What she did the whole time we were going out. She plays games. Fucks with your mind. That's one of the reasons I like you so much.' He strokes my cheek affectionately.

'What, because I'm so simple?'

He snorts. 'No.' He spins me around on the bed and hovers over me. 'But you are adorable.' He kisses my cheek. 'And straightforward.' He kisses my other cheek. 'And sexy.' His kisses start trailing down my neck. Okay, now I'm starting to feel wanted.

A cough makes both of us look towards the door. Standing there is the estate agent.

'Um...so any thoughts on the property?'

Chapter 12

Tonight is my hen do. Nadine, Kelly and Mia explained to me in the car that we're starting off with a meal in a nice restaurant and then we're hitting a club. Sounds perfect to me. I hate how most people drag it out over a whole weekend.

When we walk into my favourite restaurant, faces jump up and down screaming 'surprise.' God, the other diners are going to hate us.

I kiss hello to my co-workers, Mum and Joan. That's when I see her. His Mother. My mood plummets instantly. Great, *she's* here. That's just what I need.

She waves over, attempting to be friendly, but her eyes tell a different story. Her eyes look at me like I'm a money-hungry whore.

'Oh Florence,' she says, walking over to me. 'Can I have a little word please?'

Urggh. What the hell could she have to say to me that is

in any way nice? Surely she wouldn't want to upset me this early in the evening...could she?

'Of course,' I say, matching her fake smile.

She leads me over to a quiet corner. 'There's still time, you know.'

I frown. 'Time for what?' Does she mean starters?

She looks through me as if I'm nothing but an inconvenience. 'To back out of this farce. This so-called engagement.'

'Huh?'

She narrows her eyes at me as if she can actually shoot out ice with them.

'I have no idea how you've managed to hook my son in. God knows, you must have a magic vagina, but my son has been through a lot the last year.'

Jesus, this woman is vile.

'I know he has,' I retort, smug that I know all about it. God, if I hadn't, I'd have been mortified.

'Then you'll know that he doesn't need some money-grabbing whore getting her claws into him.'

My mouth drops open. How can she openly be this bitchy to her future daughter in law?

'Just because I haven't signed the prenup? I'll sign it if it stops you being this vindictive. But for some reason, I have a feeling this is just your personality.'

Her teeth clench together. 'Why don't we just skip the whole wedding and I'll write you a cheque right now for a million? Hmm?'

Is she for real? What kind of person does that? Tries to pay someone off?

I sigh, feeling completely defeated. 'What the hell do I have to say to make you believe I'm not after Hugh's money?'

'The money is only half of it. You're not Hugh's type.'

As if his Mother would have any idea what floats his boat. But I know what she means. I'm not from the right stock. That's what rich people say, isn't it? Make us all sound like horses. Weirdos, the lot of them.

'Err, shouldn't *he* be the one to know his type? Not his mother.' I smile, challenging her.

'His type is Felicity.' It's like taking a bullet to the heart. 'And they'd still be together if Felicity hadn't lost her mind in her grief. She's from proper stock.'

What did I tell you? Stock! Weird. So basically— because she was brought up with money, that makes her better than me. I have no idea how that logic works. If anything, surely it just produces spoilt princesses?

'Jesus, we're not horses!' I bark, my voice exploding with pent up frustration. 'And anyway, the only thing I'm after from your son is a long and happy marriage.'

'Good luck,' she sneers with a glare. 'Hugh likes the *idea* of marriage, but the reality will hit him like a freight train. Get ready to accept some affairs.'

'What?'

I hate that she's shocked me into doubting anything, but

the thought of Hugh cheating on me feels like someone has physically stabbed me in the stomach. I wonder if his Dad has ever cheated? Maybe he's seen it growing up and just thinks it's acceptable, as long as the woman doesn't find out or agrees to turn a blind eye.

She smirks—clearly pleased she's shocked me. 'You don't *honestly* think you'll be able to keep him happy forever, do you?'

'Err...that's kind of the idea of marriage.'

She gets her chequebook out and starts scribbling. 'Whatever. I'm not staying here for this poor excuse of a hen night. Here is the cheque. Think about it.' She thrusts it into my hand and turns on her heel, storming out of the main door.

'What the hell was that all about?' Mia asks her hand on my shoulder.

'Oh, not much,' I shrug sarcastically. 'Just her offering me a million to not marry Hugh.'

The girls' solution was to get me plastered, and I kindly obliged. Knowing that it's also Hugh's stag do tonight has me uneasy. Especially with these worries that he'd cheat when we're married. That means he wouldn't think twice about shagging some slag tonight. God, just the thought of any whore's hands on him makes me mad with rage.

'Flo!' Kelly says, snapping her hands in front of me. 'Snap out of it!'

'Yeah,' Nadine agrees, pushing me towards a club. 'You need to be awake to take in this place.'

I look up. It just looks like a normal nightclub.

'Why, what's wrong with it?' I ask with a frown.

'Mia booked it,' she says accusingly.

I look to Mia. She sighs. 'Okay, so it's kind of a metal night. But trust me, you'll love it!'

Metal? What the hell was she thinking? If I get crushed in a mosh pit, I'm *totally* holding her responsible.

'I think it sounds fab,' Joan says, her cheeks flushed from drinking too much wine.

'Just try to keep an open mind,' Mia warns, before flouncing in ahead.

We all follow her like lost little sheep. It's actually not as scary as I thought it would be. Yes, the place is full of alternative and goth-like people, but they're all smiley, dressed up in cheeky Christmas outfits. In the main room, there's a huge ball pit and three bouncy castles. Now I can see why Mia booked it. I love this shit! I run and dive straight into the ball pit.

We spend the next few hours drinking copious amounts of cocktails, bouncing around and exploring the different music rooms. According to Mia, I'm into Ska and Punk Regaee, whatever that means.

As the four of us walk the streets of London at four in the morning looking for a kebab shop, I can't help but feel completely grateful for my friends and family. They're the reason being single has never been too hard. With them on my side, my life has never been short of hilarious.

'Fucking fab night,' Kelly says, drool coming out of the side of her mouth.

'I'm a total metalhead!' Nadine screams, doing the metal sign with her hand.

'Calm down, dickhead,' Mia laughs. 'My people would *never* accept you as one of their own.'

Oh god. Now I really need to pee.

'Toilet. Need,' I say, clearly unable to speak in full sentences.

Nadine looks around. Her pupils are huge. They're like little flying saucers. Haha, I used to love those sweets. I wonder if there really are flying saucers. If there are such things as aliens. Shit, one of my besties could be an alien for all I know!

'Everywhere is closed, babe,' Nadine says.

When did her eyes get so weird? I cower away from her suspiciously. If anyone's an alien, it's her. With her creepy organisational skills. It's completely un-human.

'Get away from me,' I shout, pushing her away weakly. 'Alien imposter!'

'Babe,' Mia shouts, 'you're gonna have to pee behind this dumpster.'

Ugh. I don't want to be one of those girls who pees in public. Oh God, but my bladder is screaming at me. I run around it and pull up my dress and my knickers down. I squat and release the wee. God, that feels like heaven.

'I'm not this kind of girl!' I shout back at them. 'I'm a classy bitch!'

Raucous laughing suddenly explodes from behind me. I turn, still with my knickers down to see a stag do in matching green T-shirts laughing hysterically at me.

'Arggh!' I scream, running over to the girls. It's hard to run with my knickers still around my ankles, and I end up falling face down.

Nadine and Kelly try to pick me back up. 'Not, you, you alien!' I yell at Nadine. 'I know that you're not my Nadine! She's far nicer than you!'

'Shit, Flo. Calm the fuck down,' Kelly berates.

I look down at my bloody knees, the sight of it making me queasy. I suddenly feel woozy. My eyes roll back before it all goes black.

Chapter 13

Sunday 18th December

I wake up with a start, kicking my legs out of the bed. The disproportion of balance makes me topple out of it, hitting my face on the floor. My knees also sting like motherfuckers.

'Fuck,' I moan into the carpet.

How much did I drink last night?

Mia, Kelly and Nadine are passed out in different spots on the floor. I crawl, careful not to touch my knees on the floor, back into bed and put the duvet over my head. Any kind of daylight is hurting my eyes.

My phone beeps from somewhere distant. I peep out of the duvet at my bedside table. It's not there. It beeps again, and I work out that it must be still in my bag near Nadine.

I begrudgingly crawl out of bed before remembering about my bloodied knees. I still can't stand so I do a sort of backwards crab walk towards the bag. God, I'm exhausted. Every limb in my body aches. I must have danced all night. I don't actually remember getting home.

I unlock my phone to see two WhatsApp messages from a number I don't know. Oh God, I hope I didn't give my number out last night to any randoms.

I open it up to see a video attachment. Underneath it is written

I thought you should know

Know what? God, what time is it? I click on the video, cursing it for taking so long to load. When it does, cheesy Christmas music blares out of the speakers. I quickly try to turn down the volume so as not to wake the others.

I look closer, and it's a man and a woman dancing. Wait, that's red hair. Is that Felicity? They turn ever so slightly, and I see that it's Hugh. Shit. He's slow dancing with Felicity? Is this what he spent his stag night doing? As the song ends and another one starts they kiss.

It's like someone's punched me in the stomach and thrown acid at my face. He's kissing her? His old girlfriend, Felicity? What a bastard.

Something drops onto my phone screen, and it's only then I realise I'm crying. I suppose I would be upset. And this upset, under all of this numbness. It must be my body's way of protecting itself.

Nadine's eyes open slowly. She seems to take in my crying form, frowning.

'What's up?'

'It's Hugh,' I sob. 'He's cheated on me.'

We agreed yesterday for him to come to mine tonight for dinner. But that was before he decided to be a cheating bastard. For all I know he's half way to Barbados with Felicity by now, not giving me a second thought.

It's given me time to stew. I can't believe he's been this much of a selfish bastard. He's been lying the whole time. Of course, I was just collateral damage in his plan to win back Felicity. Hey, I bet it was a bonus for him that I was willing to shag him in the meantime. Fucking arsehole.

He knocks on my door at eight pm sharp. Right on time. On time to get a new arsehole ripped in.

'Hey,' he grins when he sees me. 'How was last night?' He bounds past me up the stairs.

'Pretty uneventful compared to yours, I bet,' I practically snarl.

I shut my flat door behind him.

'That's weird,' he muses, looking at the pristine kitchen. 'I thought we were gonna have dinner. Or are you so wrecked we're getting a takeaway? I don't mind either way, but I'm starving.'

How can he be acting so cavalier when only last night he had his tongue down Felicity's throat?

'Really?' I growl, leaning on one hip. 'Didn't eat enough of Felicity's face last night?'

He frowns, his eyes darting from side to side. 'What the hell are you talking about?'

'I know,' I fume, walking past him. I can't even bear to look at him, and I need to keep moving. I have so much rage coursing through my body I'm sure that if I stay still, I'll physically burst into flames.

'Know *what?* What the fuck are you going on about? I didn't even see Felicity last night.'

'Your first lie!' I snap, pointing my finger at him accusingly. 'I know that you kissed.'

He looks back at me as if I'm mad. Stupid bastard doesn't realise that I have proof.

'Who told you that?'

I fold my arms across my chest. 'An anonymous source.'

'And you believed them?' he asks in a tight voice. 'Fuck, Florence, do you not know me at all? I'd never cheat, let alone on you.'

'*Really?* Why don't I believe you?' I challenge, glaring at him.

He smiles sadly, and his shoulders sagged in defeat. 'I suppose you're right. Why am I thinking you'd have any faith in me? I've only given you no reason not to believe me. But I suppose we really don't know each other so well after all.'

'I guess you're right,' I agree with a nod. I feel the sudden pricking of tears.

He looks at me with such hurt, as if visibly wounded. Why is it I'm starting to feel bad? But no, he's the one in the wrong.

He storms out of the flat, slamming the door behind

him.

If he's the one in the wrong, then why is it I feel so lousy?

Chapter 14

Monday 19th December

I didn't sleep at all last night. I feel awful, which is ridiculous. This is his fault, his mistake. So why do I feel so lousy? Just remembering the hurt in his eyes is enough to make my stomach twist. I mean—could I have been wrong? But no, what am I thinking? I saw it on film. There's no denying that. I have physical evidence. It was him.

Maybe he was so smashed he doesn't remember, but that's not an excuse. Maybe she took advantage of him; the devious bitch. Or maybe he just saw his ex-fiancée that briefly carried their child, and realised that he still loved her? Oddly enough, I can actually understand it. I feel like I shouldn't stand in the way of their love story. It's just a shame that I got a taste of how good it could be.

The worst thing is, I knew as I was tossing and turning that the one thing to get me to sleep would be Hugh himself, fucking the life out of me. That's another thing I'm going to have to get used to. No more sex. Dammit, why did I let myself get used to feeling so good? I should have known it was too good to be true.

My doorbell rings. A bud of hope springs to life in my stomach. Oh my God, is that him? Here to apologise and beg for forgiveness? I rush to the intercom.

'Hello?' I say, my voice wobbly.

'It's us,' Kelly says, cheerful as ever. Doesn't she realise my life is in tatters?

I buzz them up without another word, leaving the door open. I fall back into bed. They better have brought comfort food.

'Morning, lover!' Kelly says, bright as a button.

'We brought pizza,' Nadine adds, clearly knowing better than to try and be cheerful.

That's enough to get me to look up. Mia's here too.

'Hey, bitch,' she smiles sadly.

I put my hand out dramatically. 'Give me.'

They open up the pizza box and hand me a slice of meat feast. I basically swallow it whole.

'Flo,' Mia says carefully, 'you have it wrong about Hugh.'

How the hell would she know?

'Oh, *really?* He's been trying to talk you round, has he? Swarmy, charming bastard.'

'No, it's not that. Look.' She pulls out her phone, and presses play.

It's a video of Troy and Jace drunkenly talking crap.

'Is this supposed to be making me feel better?' I ask in

143

confusion.

'No,' Nadine says, leaning in. She points to behind them. 'Look in the background.'

I focus in on the area and can make out Hugh and Felicity dancing again. It's like another blow to the heart. Why the hell would they want to show this to me again? Haven't I been through enough?

'How the hell is this supposed to be making me feel better?' I whine, feeling visibly wounded. 'I don't want to see them making out again!' I throw myself back down in bed and under the covers.

'No,' Mia insists, lifting the cover off me. 'This wasn't last night. The video they sent you, it's from last Christmas.'

I narrow my eyes at her. 'Huh?'

'Troy told me. It's from a Christmas party they all went to together last year.'

Could that be true? But then he'd obviously try to get his friend out of it.

'Of course Troy is going to lie for his friend,' I retort, completely unimpressed with this new information.

'He's not like that,' Mia says protectively.

We all turn to stare at her. It's not like her to give someone else the benefit of the doubt. Is something going on with them?

'How would you know?' I ask, a smile creeping on my face.

'I wouldn't,' she snaps quickly. We all share amused

144

grins. 'But this is on Troy's Instagram, dated last year. Look at the clothes Hugh and Felicity are wearing. Exactly the same as in the video you have. If you listen back to it, it's even the same song playing in the background.'

I press play again, and she's right. Shit. Could I really have been duped?

'So whoever sent the video did it purely to upset you, knowing it wasn't really last night. Who would do that?' Kelly asks.

'Duh!' I snap. 'It's obviously Felicity herself. She wants to cause problems between us.'

Now I feel awful. The hurt in Hugh's eyes was real. I've potentially just ruined the best thing that happened to me. There I was, willing to stand back and let Felicity claim him again—when in reality she's a sneaky bitch.

I stand up, pizza in hand. 'Shit, why did you let me eat this?' I shriek, trying to work out the calories I've just practically inhaled. 'I have to fit into a wedding dress in 6 days?!'

'So you're going after your man?' Kelly asks, clapping excitedly. Bless her—she watches too many rom coms. But yeah, I'm going to have to go after him and beg for forgiveness.

'Yep.' I grab my coat.

'Woah!' Nadine says, standing up and stopping me in my tracks. 'If you plan to grovel you're going to have to shower. You look like shit.'

I look down at myself. Greasy hair, still in pyjamas, which have been rolled up to let my cut knees start to heal.

'You're right. Let's get glam.'

~

An hour later I'm groomed to perfection. It helps when you have a team of three working on you. I've figured out what I'm going to say and I'm really hoping he's going to be reasonable and take the time to listen to me. See that it was a simple mistake and what the hell was I supposed to think?

I buzz up to his flat.

'Hello?' he says, sounding lame.

'Hi, it's me,' I say, my voice high-pitched and wobbly. Shit, I'm already struggling to hold it together. 'Please let me up.'

He buzzes within seconds. That's a good sign. He's letting me in.

When the lift pings I find Hugh stood outside of his door. Shit. Is he not even going to let me in? It seems I was a bit too optimistic at being let into the building.

'Hi,' I say awkwardly, not sure whether I should go in for a kiss or not.

'Hi,' he croaks. He looks like shit. His shoulders are slumped. It strangely makes me feel good. He's been just as miserable as me. There's still hope. Not that he doesn't still look edible in jeans and a black t-shirt.

'Can we go inside?' I ask, eager not to play this out in the public hallway.

'Let's just talk here.'

Great. He wants to torture me.

'Oh...okay.' I swallow in an attempt to push down my nerves. 'Look, I'm so so sorry I accused you of that. You're right, you've never given me reason to doubt you before, but I was sent a video of you both kissing.'

His forehead crinkles. 'A video?'

I nod. 'That's why I wasn't willing to listen. Because I'd seen it with my own eyes, I was so sure you'd fucked me over. Your own Mother told me it wouldn't work between us. And if I'm honest, I suppose I've been waiting for something to come and ruin this. It just seems too good to be true.'

He sighs, hands in his jean pockets. 'But you wouldn't even let me explain.'

'You rushed out of there!' I take a deep breath to try and calm myself down. I don't want to go off track here. 'Anyway, Troy explained that it was a video from last year.'

He seems to process this. 'Okay, that makes more sense. But who the hell sent it?'

'Your guess is as good as mine,' I say vaguely, not wanting to bring up Felicity. 'But I don't want them to win.'

'Neither do I,' he says, grabbing me by my waist. 'I've been miserable without you.' He tilts his forehead so it's pressing against mine. 'Promise me, next time you'll hear me out before jumping to conclusions.'

'I promise,' I nod, with a relieved smile. 'But I'm hoping there's not a next time.' I look at the door behind him. 'Now, shall we get a cheeky takeaway to celebrate our first proper fight?'

'No!' he shouts, suddenly panicked. 'Let's go out to eat. I'll just grab my wallet.'

'Okay,' I smile, joining him on walking inside.

'You stay here.'

Right, there's something going on here, and I don't like it.

'Why don't you want me to come in?' I question, sounding far too suspicious.

'No reason,' he shrugs, obviously trying to play it down. At least I know he's a shit liar.

'You won't mind if I go in then.' I barge past him into the flat, attempting to prepare myself for what finds me.

It's silent inside, but as soon as I enter, I see Felicity sitting on the sofa, her jacket off, showing off her bouncy tits in a skin-tight dress.

What. The. Fuck.

A blast of anger blindsides me, the blood drains from my face, and I boil with fury in my stomach.

'What is she doing here?' I demand, my voice erupting in an angry growl.

'Hi, Florence,' she smiles, her blue eyes flashing a quick look of hatred before she recovers to appear genuinely friendly in front of Hugh. I know it's just an act now.

She was clearly waiting to swoop in and comfort Hugh once I dumped him. With her big breasts. What a two-faced bitch.

I look at Hugh, expecting some kind of explanation. Instead, he's just biting his lip, looking ridiculously guilty.

'I can't fucking believe this,' I say, seething internally.

I storm out and head straight for the stairs. I don't have time to wait for the lift. I need to run, to keep moving. Run away from this nightmare. We have our first argument about Felicity and what does he do? Invites the brazen bitch round for wine!

'Florence, wait!' he shouts, running down the stairs after me. 'Just fucking wait!'

'Leave me alone, dickhead,' I shout back scathingly, trying to concentrate on the steps in front of me.

He catches up to me on a small landing, grabbing my arm, forcing me to turn round and face him.

'I can't believe you,' I snarl. With a sudden surge of fury, I throw him away from me. 'Having her round for a cosy chat when I'm at home, heartbroken.'

His face twitches at the word heartbroken. I suppose we haven't declared our undying love for each other or anything. Just, you know, planning on spending the rest of our lives together.

'She just turned up!' he shoots back, dragging his hand through his hair. 'We were just talking.'

'Yeah,' I scoff, 'about how you should get back together, no doubt!'

'No!' He narrows his eyes at me looking unrepentant. 'She was just being a concerned friend. You need to get this idea of us together out of your head.'

'How can I, when you have so much history, and she's still so involved in your life?'

'Look, I think us getting married has shocked her, that's all. It has shocked everyone, hasn't it.'

He's so clueless. Why is it men are so stupid?

I roll my eyes. 'If it was so innocent then why hide her inside? Why try and keep it a dirty secret?'

'Because I knew you'd jump to conclusions, just like you have!'

I cross my arms over my chest. Dammit, I hate when he's right.

I sigh, a fat tear escaping down my cheek with no warning. 'How can you not see that she wants you back?'

He sighs, exasperated. 'Even if she does, I'm not interested. I'm with you, not her. I'm marrying you, not her. I love you, not her.'

My eyes bulge out at the word love, and within a second it's like he's realised what he's said too, as his eyes mirror mine.

'You...love me?' I ask, glancing down at the floor so I don't have to look at him while he denies it. Calls it a slip of the tongue.

I hear an inhale of breath. 'Yes, I fucking do.'

I look up in disbelief. His eyes lock deeply into mine, so intense it's as if I can feel them burning.

Within a second it's as if there's no argument. It's just him and me in this stairwell, him declaring his love for me. I've never felt so fucking turned on in my life.

I crush my lips against his, suddenly desperate to have him close to me. It's been too long since I've felt his warm body crushed up against mine. He runs his hands through my hair, deepening the kiss until it's hard to breathe. I tremble, ready to melt with the heat roaring through our bodies.

He hikes up my skirt and rips my knickers clean off. Shit, he's so strong. He's like Tarzan on steroids. And Jane is just about to get it. I shiver with excitement.

He sticks a finger straight up inside me with no preamble. I gasp from the feeling of fullness, the gasp quickly turning into a groan. My hands find the top of his jeans and unbutton them, springing his erection free. I stroke it through his boxers, making him hiss with delight.

His kisses travel down my neck, before sticking a second finger inside, his thumb circling on my clit. Shit, if he carries on like this I'm going to come right here on the spot.

I don't want that. I want him inside me. Now. I yank his boxers down and fight for his jeans to follow. He lifts me up, my legs automatically wrapping around his waist. God, I can feel his dick so close to my entrance, it's like I can taste it. I need to be connected to him again, to fuck away all of this misery.

I assume he's going to throw me down on the floor but instead he places my bottom on the handrail. Woah! I grab onto his T-shirt; sure I'm going to fall to my death.

'Argh!'

'Don't worry,' he growls huskily. 'I've got you.'

At that moment, I believe him. I'd trust him with my life. He loves me. And more than anything I need him right now, more than I need to consider my safety.

He locks eyes with me and keeps intense eye contact while he thrusts into me fast, causing my bottom to almost fall over the edge.

'Shit!' I shout, grabbing onto his T-shirt.

I scramble my hands up to wrap them around his neck, desperate not to fall. If I were feeling sensible, I'd tell him this isn't safe, but I'm too fucking turned on right now. His thrusts are hard and demanding, his biceps bulging from the force of holding me in place. He seems completely confident that I'm not going to fall.

'You are mine,' he growls, making me ache to taste those lips again.

I chastely kiss his neck before placing one arm out and using it to wrap myself round the bannister. He takes this as encouragement, and his thrusts become more demanding and urgent. I feel my body start to turn to jelly, every nerve ending quivering frantically.

I hold on tighter than ever, sure me coming will result in my death. But it's like the thrill of it is making everything more intense, all the blood is rushing to my head.

Before I know it, I'm shaking my head around like a desperate whore screaming his name at the top of my lungs. I almost let go of both him and the railing, but he grips me tighter, so tight I fear I'll bruise. He grunts and stills, finding his own release.

His head collapses onto my shoulder, his laboured breaths mirroring my own.

'Fuck,' he groans, slowly pulling out of me and placing me down on my unsteady feet.

'Yeah,' is all I can say, my mind still reeling. Fuck, that was amazing.

'Come on,' he says, taking my hand, his eyes glowing with mischief. 'Let's go and tell Felicity to piss off home so we can do that all night.'

I think I can safely say that the wedding's back on.

Chapter 15

You should have seen Felicity's face when we arrived back at the apartment, clothes ruffled, my hair well and truly fucked, lipstick smudged. If I wasn't sure before, now I know she regrets dumping him. She was in equal parts horrified and jealous. Ha. He's mine bitch.

We spent the night snuggled up in front of his roaring fire watching Christmas movies and having mind-blowing sex. It was actually the happiest I can ever remember myself being.

I wake up next to him on the rug, a blanket pulled over us, the last embers of the fire going out. It makes me realise I don't care where we live. As long as I have him. And okay, maybe a fireplace.

'Morning,' he croaks, his eyes still closed.

'You want a coffee?' I ask, getting up, my own need for coffee driving me.

'I knew there was a reason I was marrying you,' he grins,

slapping my arse as I stand up.

'I think last night proved that's not the only reason,' I add with a cheeky wink.

He smiles lazily, rolling over onto his stomach so he can watch me boil the kettle stark naked.

'I have a surprise for you today.' A mischievous devastating smile re-arranges his features.

A flutter of excitement flies around my stomach. 'Really? What?'

'If I told you it wouldn't be a surprise.' He looks at his watch. 'So I hate to say it, but get dressed, we have somewhere to be.'

An hour later we're walking into a stylish industrial-looking coffee shop round the corner from Hugh's apartment.

'This is the big surprise?' I ask, looking round. 'Fancy coffee?'

'It's not the place,' he smiles. 'Its who we're meeting.'

'Riiiight. And that is?'

'It's a surprise,' he grins. He notices something behind me. 'Ah, here he is.'

I look up to see a man in his late fifties, early sixties approaching us. I rack my brains for who this could be. Another estate agent with the perfect house?

'Florence?' he says, staring right at me with a strange intensity.

I look to Hugh, confused, then back at the stranger. 'Um...sorry, but who are you?'

'Florence,' Hugh says, looking perplexed. 'Don't you recognise him? He's your father.'

I look back at the stranger in front of me. My father? My Dad that walked out on me all those years ago?

'It's so good to see you, sweetheart,' the stranger says with a broad smile.

I look back to Hugh, wanting him to protect me from this man.

'Hugh, you've got it wrong. I don't know this guy.'

'Well,' the stranger starts, 'you were young when I left. God, you look so much like my mother.'

Eww. What the actual fuck? This is him? This is the abandoner?

'Sorry, so *you're* the fucker that up and left my mum and me when I was young?'

He sighs, clearly the emotional reunion he foresaw not happening.

'There was a lot more to it than that.'

'Yeah,' I snarl sarcastically. 'I'm sure there was. Something far more important than the thought of us struggling to keep a roof over our head while you were off wherever doing God knows what.'

He looks to Hugh, flummoxed. 'I thought you said she wanted to see me?'

I stare at Hugh aghast. How could he do this to me?

'Er...I may have embellished slightly,' he admits, avoiding eye contact. 'But I figured you'd both want to see each other. You know, find out answers.'

I nearly boil over with rage. How dare he do this behind my back? Bring someone back into my life that only ever caused me upset every time I thought about them?

'I'm not fucking interested in anything this piss stain wants to say. Or his stupid excuses.' I turn to Hugh feeling nothing but rage. 'I can't believe you've done this to me.'

I get up and run out of the shop and don't stop until I'm half way down the road, bent over with a stitch. Fuck, I really need to take up running, but with these cuts still healing it's not going to be anytime soon.

'Florence! Wait!'

Why is this like Deja fucking Vu? Him upsetting me and me running away. I don't want this to become a habit.

I turn, out of breath and shove him back as far as I can. He stumbles back, his face alight with shock.

'You fucking bastard!' I yell, so loud some people in the street turn to stare.

He frowns. 'I'm so sorry, Flo. I had no idea you'd react like this. I thought you'd be happy.'

'Happy that you've found the man that abandoned me?' I snap, giving him the hardest look I can muster. 'You're supposed to protect me from things like this. From people doing me harm, but instead, you're trying to shove him in my face?'

He takes my hands, assumingly so I can't flounce off again.

'I'm so sorry, Flo. I just figured that it was every girl's dream for her Dad to walk her down the aisle. I thought you'd have loads of unanswered questions for him.'

'Well, I don't,' I cry, a tear trickling down my cheek. 'I don't give a shit about him. Anyone that left me like that doesn't deserve my time, and you should appreciate that.'

He frowns, pain in his eyes. 'I'm so sorry. Forgive me, please.'

I nod, brushing away another tear. The truth is that I need the one person who can make me feel better and that ironically happens to be the person that did this. He pulls me into his chest, rubbing my back in relaxing circles.

'I'm so so sorry, Flo. I didn't know.'

'Now you do.'

Chapter 16

We're at the pub today, making it beautiful. It's not an easy feat. Luckily Nadine has taken control of the situation and is bossing everyone around with a clipboard in her hands. I'm a little overwhelmed whenever I think of all that needs to be done in just three days, but she keeps telling me to go home. That she doesn't need me.

'Nadine's right, babe,' Hugh says, wrapping his hands around my waist. 'You're just stressing being here. Why don't you go home and chill?'

'I'll die of boredom.'

He smiles like he finds me adorable. 'My Mum and Nan are going out for lunch today. Why don't you join them?'

Is he serious? Willingly spend time with his Mother?

'I think I'll pass,' I snort. 'I doubt your Mum wants me anywhere near her.'

He frowns. 'Don't say that. I spoke to her last night, and I think she's finally accepted it.'

I laugh cruelly. 'That's like saying Cruella De Vil suddenly likes puppies.'

'Hey,' he says softly, giving me a hard look. 'You're making her out to be far worse than she is. I really don't want you guys to be at war at the wedding.'

'Too late,' I say dryly, staring heavenward.

He tilts his head to one side. 'Seriously. Can you at least *try* to get on?'

'I'm sorry, but I can't pretend.'

He sighs. A long, drawn out sigh. 'Why not?'

This is it. The time I have to choose whether to tell him about his Mum's indecent proposal or not. Fuck it. I'm not protecting her and making myself look like I have a grudge for no reason.

'Because she offered me money not to marry you, that's why!' I shout, my voice exploding in pent up frustration.

Everyone turns round to stare at me. Oops, I obviously spoke too loud.

He takes my elbow, his face like thunder, and guides me to the corner of the room.

'She did what?' he hisses.

'She offered me a million to leave you alone.'

A flash of anger passes across his face. So angry that I feel a sudden fearful thrill. 'I'll fucking kill her!' he yelps, slamming his fist into the wall.

'Shit! Calm down,' I whisper-hiss.

Dammit, I shouldn't have told him. I knew he'd go

mental. What the hell was I thinking? What bride makes her husband to be this furious three days before the wedding?

He storms off, hitting anything in his way. Thankfully that's just artificial Christmas trees.

'What the hell has happened?' Nadine asks, rushing in, bringing a gust of cold wind with her.

'I told him about his mum offering me the money.'

'Shit.' She grimaces. 'I think you should have kept it quiet.'

Where was she five minutes ago?

'It's a bit bloody late to be giving me that kind of advice!'

Chapter 17

Friday 23rd December

Hugh hasn't mentioned his Mum since yesterday. I haven't brought it up for fear of him losing it again. With only two days until we get married I really don't want to push him over the edge. It'd be pretty embarrassing if he lost it and backed out now.

Not that it seems to have mattered. I've just taken my second phone call telling me that something's wrong. First of all, the florist told me she couldn't get the flowers I'd picked out and would have to improvise, then the pub rang and said they couldn't get Hugh's favourite Peroni in stock with it being so close to Christmas. He's seriously pissed.

'Can't even have a Peroni on my wedding day. What the fuck else can go wrong?' he whines, almost to himself, busying himself in the kitchen.

'I know,' I agree, standing on my tiptoes behind him to rub his broad shoulders. 'But it's not the end of the world.'

'Really?' he asks, turning round to face me. 'I'm glad

you said that because they rang earlier and said they were out of Prosecco too.'

I grit my teeth. 'WHAT?'

His eyes crease. 'Only joking.'

I punch him on the shoulder. 'That's not even funny!'

'Oh, it is,' he grins, kissing me on the shoulder. I get a shiver of excitement every single time he touches me affectionately. I hope that continues through our marriage.

'I'm just hoping nothing else goes wrong.' My eyes wander towards the kitchen window. Oh my god. Is that...snow? 'Oh my god.'

'What?' he asks, his eyes following mine. Realisation dawns on him. 'Oh shit. That could cause more problems.'

I slump down dramatically onto the kitchen floor. 'It's all going to shit. The love pixies are against us!'

He squats down next to me, a sparkle of delight running through his face. 'Do you think you might be being a teeny, tiny bit dramatic?'

I pout like a petulant child. 'No.' I can't help but smile back at him. 'Coming from the man who was just having a hissy fit over his Peroni.'

'Dare I mention the Prosecco again?' he warns, giving my shoulder a playful shove. 'Anyway, I have the perfect thing to take our minds off it.'

'I bet you do, big boy,' I purr as seductively as I can.

He grins. 'Not that, my little minx. We're going out to play in the snow.'

I roll my eyes. 'I doubt it's even settled yet.'

'I won't have any of that whinging,' he snaps. 'And I'm calling Nadine asking that she take over all disasters from now until the wedding.'

Just, pass on all our problems to Nadine. That'll calm me down, not having any idea what's happening with my own wedding.

'But what if something truly awful happens?'

He frowns down at me. 'Then she'll call us.'

He takes my hand and drags me into the lift. He pulls my hips into his, a wicked grin on his lips. 'We're going to have to christen this lift at some point too.'

My lady parts tingle at just the idea.

'So...did you chat to your Mother the other day?' I ask as casually as I can.

He nods sternly. 'Yes. I told her she wasn't welcome at the wedding.'

'What?' I gasp, mouth hanging open. I mean, I knew he was going to go mad at her, but banning her from the wedding is a bit much. She's still his Mother.

'I don't know why you're surprised,' he says with a frown. 'I thought you'd be happy.'

'That you've fallen out with your Mother because of me? Of course that doesn't make me happy.'

The lift pings open.

'The decisions been made now, so it's over and done with,' he says finally.

Why don't I believe him? Surely deep down he'd want his mum there at his wedding?

He drags me out into the snow, which is coming down surprisingly thick. We only have the car park to play in, but we still manage to have fun, pelting each other with snowballs, using the cars for cover.

When we finally make it upstairs we strip off, have a boiling hot shower together and okay, maybe a bit of slippery sex, and then get changed into our pj's. Well, I do. He puts on a T-shirt and jogging bottoms. Then we decide to make a fort out of cushions from the sofa.

'I can't wait to be married to you,' he says with a smile as we crawl under it.

'I am pretty awesome,' I agree.

He pushes my hair out of my eyes. 'Two days, baby. Two days until you're mine.'

'I'm already yours,' I smile, wanting nothing more than to make it official. I'm conscious that I haven't told him I love him yet and that's because when I say it, I want to really mean it. I want to feel it so sure in my bones that there's no doubt. And until then I'm saying nothing.

Chapter 18

Saturday 24th December

I can't believe I'm at my own rehearsal dinner. I can't actually understand the whole concept of a rehearsal dinner. I mean, it's not a rehearsal for the wedding. Not a practical, you stand here, I stand there, kind of thing. More a poncy meal with the wedding party to indulge in talking shit.

His Grandma insisted on it being held at a nice hotel. I think it's just cruel. Show me what we could have had if we'd have accepted the money from his Mum. Not that she's here. He was serious when he said she was banned. According to his Grandma, she's devastated.

I can't help but feel bad and responsible for it all. I know she was the one in the wrong, but still, for her to miss her own son's wedding feels like a severe punishment.

I find Hugh after the speeches. He's on the balcony, snowflakes falling around him, staring out at the already settled thick snow. He should really wear a coat.

'Aren't you cold?' I ask, rubbing my own arms as goosepimples travel up them.

'A little,' he admits reluctantly. 'You definitely shouldn't be out here.' He takes off his jacket and places it round my shoulders. It reminds me of every romantic movie I've ever seen.

'What are you thinking about?' I press, studying his thoughtful face.

He smiles, his eyes tired. 'Nothing much.'

This makes me nervous. Is he getting cold feet?

'Are you having second thoughts about tomorrow?'

He turns to me, his face horrified. 'No! Of course not.' His face drops as if realising something. 'Why, are you?'

'No!' I shout with a chuckle. 'My feet are warm. Toasty warm. Even in this snow. I was just checking.' I need to bring up his Mother, but I'm not sure how he's going to react. 'Don't you miss your Mother tonight?'

'I told you,' he snaps, bad temperedly. 'I don't want anyone here that isn't one hundred percent supportive of us.'

I put my hands up in surrender. 'Okay, okay, chill out.'

I know he's lying though. Of course, it's upsetting him that his own Mother's not here. I can see it in his eyes. He can lie to me all he likes. I already know him better than he knows himself.

'Okay. I'm just going to pop in and check on the guests.'

He smiles, his eyes already back off staring into the distance.

167

That's it. I have to see her.

~

I knock on their door as soon as I arrive, eager not to waste any more time. The maid answers the door.

'Hi, is Mrs Humphrey here?'

'Oh, she very tired.'

'That's fine,' I say, pushing past her. 'I'm sure she won't mind.'

I push into the sitting room and find her lying on the sofa in silk pyjamas. Wow. I did not expect to find her like this. So...normal.

'Florence!' she yelps, when she sees me, moving so she's sitting up. 'What are you doing here?'

I notice two empty wine bottles on the coffee table. Drowning her sorrows, clearly. Weird, because she actually looks sober. Maybe she's one of those alcoholics that doesn't actually show it.

'I'm here to have it out with you,' I explain, hand on my hip.

'Should I call police, Mrs Humphrey?' the maid asks. I turn to look at her. She flinches like I'm going to hit her.

'That won't be necessary,' she says back to her. 'This is, after all, my future daughter in law,' she says with clear distaste. 'Whether I like it or not.'

I sit down across from her. 'Look, I get that you don't like me. I'm not posh enough for you, and you're sure I'm out to steal Hugh's money, but sooner or later you're going to realise I'm here for life. I'm not a quitter, and I definitely don't plan on quitting on my marriage.'

'Please,' she scoffs. 'You don't even know each other. How can you be so confident?'

'Because I love him.'

Wow, I'm not supposed to be shocked at that myself. Do I love him? Shit, I suppose I do. That snuck up on me without me realising.

'I know how I feel, and I know how Hugh feels. I get that you doubt us, but surely in five years time, when you realise I'm still there, you're going to regret not going to your son's wedding?'

'You make it sound like a choice,' she scoffs. 'Hugh told me in no uncertain terms that I was unwelcome.'

I sigh. God, she's stubborn. 'Only because you tried to pay me off to disappear!'

'Florence, one day you may have a son. That son may very well be my Grandson. Let me tell you that you will be just as protective as me. Hugh's my only baby. I just want to make sure he's being looked after.'

'Did I take the money?' I ask scornfully, crossing my arms over my chest.

'Not yet,' she admits reluctantly. 'But it's still on the table.'

'I don't believe you!' I explode. 'Here I am, offering you an olive branch and you're still trying to piss all over it.'

She smiles sadly. I have no idea what that smile means.

I take a deep breath and try to centre myself. I'm here for Hugh, not her.

'Look, I know that deep down Hugh would really love it if you were there. Please come tomorrow.'

I can't believe I'm asking her this, but it's the right thing.

'You'd still invite me, after all I've just said?' she asks, giving me a quizzical look.

I sigh, exhausted from arguing. 'Yes.'

She muses over this for a moment. 'Then maybe I'm wrong. Maybe you are right for him.'

Wow. I never thought I'd hear that out of her mouth.

'Thank you,' I smile, grabbing at the compliment while it's still available.

'But you still have the cheque, just in case.'

She had to ruin it.

'God, you're annoying.'

~

By the time I make it back to the rehearsal dinner most people have gone. I search around for Hugh and spot him by a Christmas tree just past the lobby. He's going to be so happy when I tell him his Mum has come round and is attending tomorrow.

I attempt to wave when I see that he's talking to

someone. My hand remains hovering in the air when I notice that the person is Felicity. What the hell? I thought she hadn't turned up tonight, but now I find her talking closely to Hugh the night before my wedding?

He's frowning, deep in some discussion with her. What the hell are they talking about, alone, at this time of night? And did I mention THE NIGHT BEFORE MY WEDDING!!

She leans in and hugs him. It's like someone's winded me. I hold onto a pillar to steady myself, unable to look away. He closes his eyes shut as if her touch is causing some kind of emotional pain. She pulls back slightly and looks up at him. His eyes are pained, the internal war he's fighting, evident.

Get off him, whore.

My heart misses a beat as he slowly lowers his head. Please God, please no. Don't kiss her. His lips connect with hers.

I spin around, feeling faint. Oh my God. Oh my fucking God. He still loves her. Of course he does. I was right all along. I was just some kind of plan to bring her back to him. The callous bastard. He played me. He played me good.

I can't breathe. I slump down against the pillar, the air in the room close. My life is over. The life that we'd planned anyway, the life I'd seen myself living, all gone in one betraying kiss.

Adventurous Proposal

Chapter 19

I haven't slept a wink all night. Nadine insisted on staying over, but I haven't had the heart to tell her. I mean, once I say it out loud it's real. At least right now I can pretend I've made some kind of mistake. But I mean, how do you mistake two people kissing? They either are, or they aren't, right?

'Are you sure you're okay, hun?' Nadine asks as she places down my scrambled eggs on toast.

'Yeah,' I shrug. 'Just...nervous.'

And worrying if I should marry my cheating bastard of a fiancée.

She smiles reassuringly. 'There's nothing to be nervous about. Us guys have made that old run down pub look fabulous. I mean, it's nearly killed us, but to see your face will make it all worth it.'

I keep checking my phone to see if Hugh has tried to call me. Nothing. Maybe he's sitting in his own kitchen right now wondering if it's too late for him to run. Maybe Felicity's there with him having stayed the night. I wince my eyes shut at the idea, my stomach churns.

Perhaps I should just take his Mum's money and run. Cut my losses. Even if he does turn up today, that still means he plans to start our married life lying to each other. That he finds kissing other women to be nothing he should run by me first. I don't know what to bloody do.

I know if I tell the girls they'll be horrified and demand I don't marry him. Is it sad that I don't want them to think badly of him? And that deep down I do want to marry him. God, I'm confused. And pathetic. I suppose love does do that to people.

Do I love Hugh? God knows I've tried to keep away from saying it and not meaning it, but now the thought of not spending the rest of my life with him causes physical pain. Oh God, my head is spinning.

~

'You look stunning,' Mum gushes, staring at me in my dress.

I deliberately kept this dress a secret from the others, wanting it to be a grand reveal, and by their faces, I'd say it's worth it.

I really don't know how I've let it get this far, but I've tried to break everything down into tiny tasks. Have a shower. Go to Mum's house. Do my hair and makeup. And now I'm standing here in the dress and the car is coming to collect me in thirty minutes.

'Okay, I'm starting to freak out,' I admit, swallowing convulsively, my stomach heaving.

'I knew this would happen,' Mum says, tutting. 'Rushing in to marry someone you don't know.' She pats me on the shoulder. 'It's okay, love. It's not too late to back out.'

'Isn't it?' Mia shrieks. 'It's an hour before the fucking wedding! I've just broken my back the last few days decorating that pub!'

It's hard to find her scary when she's dressed in the ruby-red bridesmaid dress I picked for her. She looks so elegant. Even with the purple hair and black nail varnish.

'Don't shout at her,' Kelly retorts. 'She's totally entitled to a pre-wedding freakout.'

Thank God for happy Kelly. I turn to her. I need some positivity.

'Do you think I'm making a huge mistake?' I ask, not sure if I want to hear the answer.

'Of course not,' she laughs. 'You've found a rich, gorgeous man that wants to marry you. There should be no hesitation in sight. God, if you don't marry him, I will!'

'Flo,' Nadine calls from upstairs. When did she disappear up there? 'Come help me with something.'

'She's the bride, bitch!' Mia shouts up. 'She shouldn't be helping you do anything! Do your job, maid of honour!'

'I need her,' she shouts back down.

'Ugh, I'll go. Don't worry.'

I stomp up the stairs. Like I'm not having enough of a melodrama down here. She's sitting waiting for me on my Mum's bed.

'What is it?' I demand, hand on hip.

'I just wanted to get you away from the others.' She pats the bed beside her. 'Look, if you're having second thoughts, you don't have to go through with this.'

I slump down on the bed, the dress making a funny noise beneath me.

'I know,' I admit. 'I'm just so confused.'

She frowns, studying my face. 'Why? What's happened? Yesterday you were so sure.'

Trust her to see straight through me.

'I...I saw him kiss Felicity last night.'

'WHAT?' she yelps, standing up.

I jump up to quieten her. 'Sssh! I don't want anyone to know.'

She scoffs. 'What, that your fiancée is a fucking dog?!'

See, this right here is why I didn't want to tell her. I know her mind will be made up now, and she won't let me marry him.

'I don't know the full story,' I shrug.

'What is there to know?' she asks, outraged on my behalf. 'He cheated.'

'I know,' I sigh, 'but...I love him.' I feel better as soon as

I've said the words out loud.

'You do?' she asks with sad eyes. That's not normally the reaction you get from a friend when you tell them you're in love. I nod. 'That means you're going to marry him anyway, right?'

I rub my forehead, trying to gather my fumbled thoughts. 'Ugh, I don't know.'

She paces around the room a while.

'Okay, look, why don't you get married and if you find out he's a cheating arse just divorce the son of a bitch?'

I sigh. 'You know how I feel about divorce. When I say my vows, I want them to be forever.'

She rolls her eyes. 'God, you're so ridiculous.'

'Car's here, girls!' Mum calls up the stairs.

Nadine looks at me, eyes wide. 'This is it, Flo. Now or never.'

~

The car pulls up outside the pub. I force myself to take deep breaths for fear I'll forget all together otherwise. This is it. I'm marrying Hugh. So why can't I get out of the car?

'Are you okay sweetheart?' Mum asks for the millionth time.

'I just...I just...' A stray tear falls down my cheek. Dammit, I don't want to ruin my makeup.

Mia and Kelly come to the door carrying their bouquets of red roses with gardenia.

'What's the hold up, chick?' Kelly asks, smiling brightly

but with worried eyes.

Mia's applying an extra layer of red lipstick using the car window reflection. Clearly, she's not as worried.

'Where's Nadine?'

'She ran in,' Mia explains, pouting her lips to check them out. 'Said she had to ask Hugh something.'

Oh shit. What if she's gone in there all guns blazing screaming abuse at him for kissing Felicity? I have to get her. But my legs still won't move. The cold isn't helping. I shiver, covering my shoulders with my faux fur stole.

'I don't think I can go in,' I admit, my mouth chattering.

They both turn at the sound of crunching in the snow to see Hugh headed towards us with Nadine. Oh God. What has she done?

'Ladies,' he nods in greeting. 'You all look beautiful. Can I please have a word with my bride?'

Mia raises her eyebrows, but gets the hint and goes, shooing Kelly and Mum away with her. Hugh gets into the other side of the car. I tremble, not knowing what I even want to say to him.

'What's going on?' he asks as soon as we're alone.

'I feel sick,' I admit, my voice breaking.

'Do you not want to marry me?' he asks, his eyes guarded. For a brief moment, his stunning face is unexpectedly vulnerable.

'Of course I do. I just...'

'I know what you're worried about,' he says, smiling in

relief.

Oh, thank God. He knows I saw them.

'You're worried I'd be cross about you re-inviting my Mother.'

Oh god, he doesn't get it? This has nothing to do with his bloody Mother!

'Don't worry,' he smiles, taking my hand in his large one. 'Yes, I was shocked to see her this morning, but she explained how you went to her last night. I did wonder where you'd got to.'

'Did you?' I ask, the question loaded. He didn't look that way when he was kissing Felicity.

'Of course I did. I missed you.' He pulls me in for a quick kiss on the end of my nose. 'It's strange how after such a short period of time I've come to crave your company.'

I smile, my insides warming. It's easy to forget the kiss when he's saying such sweet things.

'I do too. The truth is that I realised last night that...' I take a deep breath, 'I love you.'

His mouth drops open. 'Really?'

I nod, struggling to keep my emotions under control.

'You're not just saying that because I said it to you, are you?'

'No. I realised last night.' *When you cheated on me,* I want to add.

He swallows, suddenly nervous. 'Look, while we're getting things off our chest I have to tell you about Felicity last night.'

I straighten and gulp down the bile. 'Oh?'

This is where I find out. He can either tell me a lie or the truth.

'She was pretty drunk last night and cornered me while I was looking for you. She started going on about the past and how it could be us getting married today.'

That bitch.

'Then she started bringing up the baby.' His eyes glisten over with tears. 'We were both upset.'

I'm waiting for the words to leave his mouth and pierce my heart.

'But I told her we would have never worked. Explained that I love you now. She was devastated, so I gave her one last kiss goodbye.'

'One last snog more like!' I scream, all of the pent up emotion exploding into one sentence.

'What?'

'I saw you, Hugh!' I accuse. 'I came back last night, and I saw you kiss.'

'Right,' he nods, not seeming to gather why I'm so furious. 'Then you'd have seen how I pushed her away when she tried to turn it into something it's not.'

I stare at him, trying to work out if he's lying. His eyes seem truthful.

'It was really just a kiss goodbye?'

I watch as his fingers close around mine, the connection

restoring between us.

'Flo, if I didn't want to marry you, do you really think I would be here right now?'

I suppose he is here, looking pretty bloody dashing in his morning suit. But then I think of Felicity waiting in there.

'Is she here?'

He shakes his head. 'No. I told her she wasn't welcome.'

I breathe a sigh of relief. I hadn't realised how much I was dreading seeing her smug face.

'Are we okay now?'

I smile. 'Better than ever.'

He pulls me in and kisses me sweetly. 'You look amazing by the way.'

I grin. 'Quick, go in there so I can walk down the aisle to you.'

'With pleasure, soon to be Mrs Humphreys. Wait till you see the place. You really won't recognise it.' He jumps out and crunches his way back through the snow, a new spring in his step.

Mum leans back into the car, all smiles. 'You ready, my love?'

'As I'll ever be,' I smile, getting out. My silver shoes, covered in tiny diamantes crunch against the snow. I call them my Cinderella shoes. I've never felt so much like a princess.

We walk slowly round to the back of the garden where fairy lights are glistening, guiding us towards the hall of the barn.

A man in a suit opens the door, and I get to see the amazing work my friends have done for the first time. The whole barn has been painted white, fairy lights hanging from the ceiling. Bouquets of red roses, gardenia, stephanotis and anemone sit in nearly every corner of the room. Fold up wooden chairs containing our guests are laid in rows towards the made up alter area. At the end of the rows, snow-dusted pinecones hang from red ribbon. It's bloody beautiful.

The guitar chords for James Arthur's 'Say You Won't Let Go' start playing. Goosepimples rise on my whole body as everyone stands up and turns to face me. A collective gasp fills the room as they take in my fabulous dress.

Mum smiles at me, taking my arm. We start to walk slowly down the aisle, everyone beaming back at me. I'm glad that I know about 80% of them and I'm guessing the other 20% are on Hugh's side.

This song gets me every time. Just looking at the details my friends and family have put in, together with the honey voice of James Arthur makes me feel ridiculously emotional. I look at Hugh, at the front with his men. He's smiling at me like he's made the best decision of his life. When I was a little girl that right there is how I imagined my groom looking at me.

Before I know it, I'm with him, as if I've floated down the aisle. Mum kisses me on the cheek, dabbing her eye with a tissue. She rushes off to sit with Joan who's wearing a ridiculous huge red hat with a cat on it. I quickly look back to Hugh's side and smile when I see his Mum looking proudly on, a tissue at her own eye.

The registrar starts talking, but I'm not even listening. I'm just staring into Hugh's green eyes, at the devotion in them. I know he won't let go of me. We're in this together.

I carry on through the ceremony as if in a dream. Before I know what's happened people are cheering, I have a ring on my finger and Hugh is pulling me in close to him, pressing his lips to mine hungrily. He dramatically dips me back, just like in a Hollywood movie. I giggle—the flashes of the guest's smartphones snapping away at our perfect moment.

He takes my hand and guides me back down the aisle. Everyone throws confetti over us. Some catch in the cleavage of my dress. I look down to see that it's tiny silver snowflakes. The barn doors open to reveal the same man that let me in holding out two glasses of Prosecco for us.

'Wait til you see the inside, wifey.'

God, I'm his wife. It's going to take a long time to get used to that.

I let him lead me towards the pub entrance. The door itself is wrapped in ivy. He opens it, and I gasp. This can't surely be the same pub that we saw only a few days ago?

All the old tables are covered with white tablecloths, a professional setting of plates, cutlery and glasses. The chairs are covered in white with big red sashes around them, a sprig of ivy attached to the bow. The centrepieces are the most extraordinary things I've ever seen. There's a round block of wood and on top of it is a long rectangular block of ice. Frozen inside is one single red rose. They are stunning.

'A little nod to Beauty and the Beast,' he whispers in my ear.

'You remembered?'

He winks. 'Of course I did.'

I've actually married the man of my dreams.

The knives and forks are nestled into little red Christmas stockings. They look adorable. The name place cards are held up by a silver snowflake Christmas tree bauble. Underneath them is a white organza bag with a crystal snowflake engraved with our initials and wedding date for them to hang on their tree each year. There are bottles of Prosecco standing in ice mixed with berries and ivy, on each table, ready to be poured. God, that is going to taste amazing.

Mini snow-covered Christmas trees are scattered around the room. The chalkboard has *Tis the season to be married* drawn on it in Nadine's handwriting. The cake is spectacular. Four tiers of plain white icing, red, white and silver snowflakes trailing down it.

In another corner, there's a hot chocolate bar set up, the optional toppings of whipped cream, marshmallows, chocolate drops and cinnamon wafers making me want to go over and stuff my face. Next to the cups are little fudge pieces in the shape of hearts. I know from here that they're Mum's homemade ones.

'How did you know about my Mum's fudge?' I ask, startled. I definitely didn't tell him.

'My Grandma might have mentioned it,' he says with a wink.

'I can't believe you guys did all this.'

'Anything for you.' He pecks a kiss on my cheek.

'God, you guys must have raised the value of this place by loads! What a shame they couldn't afford to do it themselves.'

He grins like he has a secret.

'What?' I ask, a smile spreading on my lips.

He puts his hands into his pockets. 'Well, I kind of bought the place.'

'You kind of WHAT?'

'The owners are struggling, and a construction company had approached them asking to buy it.'

Images of my wedding venue being turned into high-rise flats cross my mind.

'You're not knocking it down and building on it, are you?'

He smiles. 'No. That's why I bought it. I want to be able to come back here every anniversary for dinner.'

I grin. 'So you think we'll make it past a year?' I ask playfully.

He rolls his eyes. 'Of course we will! Nadine's agreed to

be the manager, so together, with the help of the old owners, we're hoping to make this into the must-have wedding venue.'

Wow. I knew Nadine had been unhappy at her job, but I had no idea this was all going on behind the scenes.

'Got big plans, hmm? Perhaps something you should have discussed with your wife?'

'You weren't my wife then,' he chuckles. 'But I promise. Nothing but the truth from now on.'

~

After a delicious meal of roast turkey with all of the trimmings and wedding cake, the same guy that gave us our drinks shouts that the evening barn is ready. I didn't realise we were going back in there. I guess I just kind of assumed we'd push some of the tables over to have a little dance.

Instead, Hugh takes my hand and leads me, the wedding party following, back towards the barn. The doors open to reveal that the folded chairs are now around the edges of the room. A DJ is set up where we said our vows, Bruno Mars' *I think I wanna Marry You* pumping out of the speakers. There are lights set up which reflect different shaped snowflakes onto the dance floor. It's bloody magical.

Hugh takes my hand, leading me to the centre of the dance floor. I wrap my arms around his neck—our bodies melded together.

'I'm so glad we did this,' he smiles. 'Easily the best

decision I've ever made.'

'I can't help but agree, dear husband of mine.'

Epilogue

I can't wait to celebrate our first anniversary tonight, at the very pub we got married in. I still can't believe what a total gold mine it's turned into. With Nadine being the driving force, the wedding business has gone from strength to strength. There's even talk of them only opening for weddings and no longer the general public.

I wrap up the last minute Christmas present for Hugh. I can't wait to see his face when he pulls out the positive pregnancy test. He's going to be over the moon. I only came off the pill two months ago.

We wanted to wait until we were settled in our new place. Soon after we'd married, we bought our dream home in the quiet commuter village of Kings Langley. It has the cutest little high street and is still only twenty minutes from London. Plus, we got so much more for our money. We managed to afford our period four-bedroom detached house. I mean, yeah, it practically had to be gutted, but with Hugh's company, it was done quickly. He made sure to keep all of the period features that made me fall in love with it.

They say the first year of marriage is the hardest. Well, I call bullshit. It feels like Hugh and I were always destined to be together. Yeah, we're still finding out lots about each other, but when it comes down to it being in love isn't about listing someone's hobbies or having loads in common. It's about the feeling you get when you look at them, the feeling of coming home. Hugh is my home, and I never plan on moving out.

Acknowledgements

First, thanks to you the reader for buying my book. You keep my child in shoes!

To my personal cheerleaders; the hubster, Mumma L and Auntie Mad. Your unfailing faith in me is what keeps me going.

I am also so appreciative for all of the people that constantly take time out of their day to promote me, whether it be bloggers or readers. I'd have no career without you guys.

Yummy by Design - I'm so grateful to have finally found a designer who totally gets me and also works up until midnight! You make my books beautiful.

Leigh Stone - Thank you for being the formatting wizard that you are! Your patience with all of my last minute changes is amazing. You are an absolute star.

To my PA's Kaprii and Lorraine, you girls are so organised and help me get my life together!

Last but not least thank you to my crazy family and friends. Without you guys I wouldn't have the love, confidence or hilarious stories I need to keep going. Love you!

Check out Laura's other titles

The Debt & the Doormat Series:

The Debt & the Doormat

The Baby & the Bride

Porn Money & Wannabe Mummy

Standalones

Tequila & Tea Bags

Dopey Women

Sex, Snow & Mistletoe

Heath, Cliffs & Wandering Hearts

Connect with Me

www.laurabarnardbooks.co.uk

www.facebook.com/laurabarnardbooks

https://twitter.com/BarnardLaura

https://www.instagram.com/laurabarnardauthor/

13204805R00111

Printed in Germany
by Amazon Distribution
GmbH, Leipzig